Malachi turned and slowly, very slowly, smiled at her.

"You see, that money didn't come from King Industries. It came from me. From my *personal* bank account. And my terms are *personal*, too."

Addie swallowed, or tried to swallow at least, past a lump in her throat.

"What do you mean by *personal*?" she croaked. Around her, the air felt hot and leaden and the room was growing darker.

"What do you mean?" she repeated and the lump felt sharp and jagged now.

His voice was soft, just as it had been when he'd promised to love and honor and cherish her forever. But the hard lines of his face were knife-sharp and harder than stone.

"I've been very patient, but you owe me a honeymoon, sweetheart."

"I—I don't understand."

His gaze swept over her slowly.

"Then let me explain. I want you to come away with me for a month. To be my mistress." His eyes locked on hers, pinning her against the leather upholstery. "Do that and you can keep the money. And who knows? There might even be a little bonus in it for you."

Louise Fuller was a tomboy who hated pink and always wanted to be the prince—not the princess! Now she enjoys creating heroines who aren't pretty pushovers but are strong, believable women. Before writing for Harlequin, she studied literature and philosophy at university, then worked as a reporter on her local newspaper. She lives in Tunbridge Wells with her impossibly handsome husband, Patrick, and their six children.

Books by Louise Fuller

Harlequin Presents

A Deal Sealed by Passion
Vows Made in Secret

Visit the Author Profile page at
Harlequin.com for more titles.

Louise Fuller

—

CLAIMING HIS WEDDING NIGHT

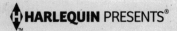
HARLEQUIN PRESENTS®

Recycling programs
for this product may
not exist in your area.

ISBN-13: 978-0-373-13462-5

Claiming His Wedding Night

First North American Publication 2016

Copyright © 2016 by Louise Fuller

www.Harlequin.com

Printed in U.S.A.

CLAIMING HIS WEDDING NIGHT

To Jane Arnold.
For Friday coffee and shopping;
for making it up to Southwold so many times;
and for being my friend.

Thank you.

CHAPTER ONE

SHE SHOULD BE PLEASED. Good publicity was what charities like hers survived on. Only it was doing more than surviving, Addie Farrell thought with a small smile of satisfaction as she glanced down at the newspaper. It was just five years since they had opened their doors to offer music to disadvantaged children in the city, but the way things were going, they might be able to open a second centre soon.

Addie frowned. The article was one hundred per cent approving—even the photograph was flattering. So why did she feel so deflated? Her smile faded. Probably because the glossy red curls tumbling over her shoulders and the nervous excitement in her blue eyes hinted at a different Addie—an Addie she had been a long time ago, for a few blissful months. The Addie she might still be now if Malachi King hadn't taken her heart and tossed it aside like some unwanted corporate gift.

Don't go there! she warned herself. The article was about her hard work and determination. It had absolutely nothing to do with her rat of an estranged husband. Or their foolhardy and doomed marriage.

That was all in the past now.

Her present—her future—was a world away from that dark place she'd slipped into after Malachi had broken her heart. And she had survived worse than his defection. Her muscles tensed as she remembered the car accident that had shattered her dream of playing the piano professionally. It had been devastating, but she had not given up and now she had the best job in the world: bringing music to children whose lives were a constant battle with poverty and neglect.

She sighed. Only that would keep happening if she got on and knuckled down to her admin.

Opening her laptop, she began clicking through her emails. Twenty minutes later she reached across the desk and picked up a pile of envelopes from her in tray. Glancing at the one on top, she felt her breath catch sharply in her throat, the beat of her heart suddenly swift and urgent. As though mesmerised, she stared blankly at the embossed logo on the front of the envelope.

King Industries. Owned by her very rich, very handsome and very estranged husband Malachi.

The blood was roaring in her ears, and for a moment she imagined tearing up the letter and hurling the pieces into the warm Miami air. And then, with hands that shook slightly, she tore it open and read the letter inside.

It took three attempts before her brain could connect the words to their meaning. Not that the letter was badly written. Quite the opposite, in fact. It was polite and succinct, informing her that, after five years of funding, King Industries would be withdrawing their financial support from the Miami Music Project.

Heart pounding, Addie scanned through the lines, her eyes inexorably drawn to the signature at the bottom of the page. Bracing her shoulders, she felt her chest squeeze tight as she stared at her husband's name.

Fury snapped through her bones like electric sparks. Was this some kind of cruel joke?

He hadn't been in touch for five years. *Five years!* Not a phone call, an email, a text.

Nothing.

This was the first time he'd contacted her since their wedding day and it was some stock letter telling her that he was cutting the funding for her charity! It was despicable! And so cowardly when he hadn't even had the guts to speak to her, let alone meet her face-to-face.

Somewhere beneath her ribs she felt something twist—a wrench, slight yet irrevocable. If she hadn't known better she might have thought it was her heart.

Her whole body was shaking and she felt a sudden spasm of helpless rage. Wasn't it enough that he'd crushed her romantic dreams? His support for her charity was the *one* good thing that had survived their marriage. Only now he wanted to wreck that too.

What kind of man would do something like that to his wife?

Her stomach cramped as she miserably remembered her wedding day, and how Malachi had promised to love her. Looking into her eyes with a shimmering heat that had made her heart quiver, he had made her believe he meant every word.

Gritting her teeth, she stared down at the face looking back up at her from the newspaper.

How could you have ever believed that he loved you?

Her face tightened. She'd known all about his reputation as a womaniser, a player of hearts as well as cards. But of course she'd believed him. Who wouldn't? That was what Malachi did best. He looked into your eyes and smiled, a gorgeous, curving smile, and he made you believe.

He made the gamblers in his casinos believe they would beat the tables.

And he'd made her believe that he loved her.

But he hadn't. Instead he had used her and exploited their relationship to improve his bad-boy image. Their marriage had been nothing more than a stunt conceived and executed by a man who had built a multibillion-dollar business by ruthlessly taking what he wanted. A man who liked playing games almost as much as he liked to win.

Her head snapped up and, lifting her shoulders, she eased her head from side to side, like a fighter about to step into the ring.

Maybe it was about time he found out what it was like to lose.

Breathing out slowly, Addie lifted up the letter and stared at it bleakly.

He might have had the 'house edge' during their relationship, but if he thought this letter would be the last word on their marriage he could think again. A lot had changed in the five years since they'd separated. She knew what lay behind his smile now, and she certainly wasn't the same lovestruck young woman he'd married.

Rapidly typing into her keyboard, she narrowed her eyes as she picked up her phone and quickly punched in the number at the top of the letter.

'Good morning! King Industries. How may I help you?'

Feeling her heart start to pound, Addie took a deep breath and said quickly, 'I'd like to speak to Mr King!'

'Could I take your name, please?'

Her shoulders stiffened. Gripping the phone tightly, she bit down hard on her lip. It was her last chance to change her mind. To leave the past sealed.

For a moment she almost hung up, and then, dry-mouthed, she closed her eyes and said hoarsely, 'Addie Farrell.'

There was a pause.

'I'm sorry, Ms Farrell, I don't seem to have you down for an appointment.'

'I don't have one,' she said, surprised and even a little impressed by the firm, even tenor of her voice. 'But it's important—vital that I speak to him!'

'I understand that, Ms Farrell.' The girl sounded young, and a little nervous. But despite her youth she had clearly been well-trained. 'And I'll do my best to help, but Mr King doesn't speak to anyone without an appointment.'

Opening her eyes, Addie cursed softly. Of course he didn't. Malachi was the CEO. His calls would obviously be screened and only the most important would be put through to him. She gritted her teeth. But who could be more important than his wife?

Somewhere at the back of her head a voice was warning her to hang up, but it was muffled by the angry, insistent beat of her heart. 'He'll speak to me,' she said slowly. 'Just give him my name.'

There was another, longer pause. 'I can't do that, Ms Farrell. But I can certainly arrange an appointment. Or if you'd like to leave a message—'

Addie smiled grimly. 'Fine,' she snapped. 'Tell him it's his wife. I just wanted to remind him that it's our wedding anniversary tomorrow.'

There was a total, frozen silence and she felt an unexpected but welcome ripple of satisfaction wash over her.

'If you wouldn't mind passing that message on? I don't mind holding,' she said sweetly.

Outside the window of his private jet an ethereal pale blue sky stretched to the horizon. It was beautiful, humbling. But Malachi King was oblivious to the view. Instead his gaze was locked to the screen in front of him, his dark grey eyes moving swiftly over the columns of figures that filled the page.

'What happened on Table Twenty-five?' he asked abruptly, looking up at the thickset, middle-aged man seated opposite him.

'There was an incident. A bunch of guys on a stag night got a bit messy. But I dealt with it. Nice and smooth, Mr King.'

'That's what I pay you for, Mike. To keep it all smooth!'

Glancing at the message on the screen of his phone, Malachi gave a small, tight smile. If only he could smooth out his parents' messy lives so easily. But unfortunately Henry and Serena King were showing no sign of giving up their decadent habits any time soon, and as their only son he had no option but to clean up after them.

There was a knock on the cabin door and both men watched in silent appreciation as a sleek brunette wearing the uniform of the King Industries private airline sashayed into the room.

'Your coffee, Mr King! Will there be anything else?'

Malachi's smile shifted. Breathing in sharply, he let his eyes linger on the almost ludicrous swell of the woman's bottom against the navy fabric of her skirt. He felt his body stir—

Will there be anything else?

Surely that was one of the advantages to owning your own plane? Sex with a beautiful woman at forty-one thousand feet? It certainly beat an in-flight movie and a packet of peanuts. He let his gaze drift over the woman's body. She was very beautiful. And desirable. But he would never sleep with her. Not only because she worked for him—that, of course, put her off limits—but because she was just too available. There was no excitement, no challenge in bedding a woman like her.

He didn't miss a beat.

'No, thank you, Victoria. Just the coffee.' His intonation was perfect, polite but neutral, making it clear that while he might remember her name that was the beginning and the end of their relationship.

He turned his attention back to his security chief. 'It all looks good, Mike. I'm going to chill for ten minutes, so enjoy the rest of the flight.' It was a dismissal, but again done with exactly the right blend of warmth and efficiency. Leaning back in his seat, he heard the door shut and, reaching forward, clicked the phone on the desk. 'No more calls, Chrissie.'

Closing his laptop, he breathed out slowly. Now he could enjoy the view!

He didn't really understand why but it was something of a guilty pleasure for him, watching the sky stretch out and away—a giant, vaulted ceiling of blue. Was it something to do with the colours? He frowned. Maybe. Or maybe it was because the serenity and calm was so unlike the chaotic debauchery of life with his parents.

He shifted in his seat, feeling it for the first time: that soft pressure, like a finger pushing against a bruise. A memory of eyes that exact colour, widening, changing from light to dark, cool to hot—eyes that set off a jangling alarm inside his head.

He gritted his teeth. He tried never to think about Addie. His wife. But this time of year, this month—tomorrow, in fact—always made him unusually tense. He had to dig deep to calm himself, to stop his nerves from ringing.

He jolted forward in his seat. The ringing wasn't inside his head. It was his phone. Mouth hardening, he stared at it in disbelief and then, frowning, snatched it up. 'This had better be good,' he said tersely. 'Or at least entertaining enough for you to have disturbed me—'

There was a short, tense silence, and then he heard his personal assistant breathe out nervously.

'I'm sorry, Mr King—I didn't want to do the wrong thing. I wouldn't have bothered you, but she said it was important so I put her on hold. Is that okay?'

She! In other words, his mother. Gritting his teeth, Malachi felt a surge of irritation. But he couldn't really blame his assistant. Serena King could make a broken nail sound like a diplomatic incident if she chose.

Imagining his mother's likely mood, he grimaced. *Please let it not be something too sordid. Or illegal.* 'It's fine, Chrissie. I'll speak to her now,' he said slowly.

Better just to take the call, for Serena would not take kindly to being fobbed off after having been kept on hold. And her unkindness was not something he wanted to provoke.

'Yes, sir.' The girl hesitated. 'And Happy Anniversary for tomorrow, Mr King!'

Suddenly his jaw was clenched so tightly he could feel his teeth vibrating. His whole body was on high alert, his mind rewinding their conversation.

There was only one other person aside from himself who knew that tomorrow was his wedding anniversary. And it certainly wasn't his mother. He'd made damn sure that his parents had been kept well away from his marriage.

He breathed out slowly. 'I think we might be speaking at cross purposes.'

Glancing down, he saw that his hand was curled tightly over the armrest, the knuckles protruding whitely against his skin. With an effort, he splayed the fingers apart.

'Who exactly have you got on hold, Chrissie?'

She cleared her throat, and when she spoke again, her voice was high and nervous. 'I—I'm sorry, Mr King,' she stammered. 'I thought you understood. It's your wife. Ms Farrell!'

Malachi stared across the cabin. Outside the window the sky had clouded over. Everything was the same pure white as newly settled snow. The same pure white as the dress Addie had worn when she'd spoken her wedding vows. His throat tightened. His motives for marrying might have been a little self-serving—even a little manipulative. But either way, she'd promised to love and cherish and honour him. Only her promises had been as fragile and tenuous as the clouds breaking apart outside the window.

Why now? he wondered. Why, after all this time, had she chosen this moment to get in touch? For a moment random thoughts collided in his head—irritation, curiosity, disquiet—and then abruptly he sat up straighter.

'What a charming surprise,' he said smoothly. 'You'd better put her through.'

The phone line clicked and his stomach tensed as, for the first time since their wedding, he heard the light, clipped voice of his wife.

'Malachi? It's me. Addie!'

'Apparently so,' he drawled softly.

It had been five years, but nothing in his manner

gave any hint of how unsettling it was to hear her again. Nor would it. Years spent playing high-stakes poker had taught him early and hard the value of never giving anything away. He grimaced. That and being Henry and Serena's son. It was just a pity he hadn't remembered that lesson when he'd first met Addie.

'It's been a long time, sweetheart,' he murmured. 'To what do I owe the honour?'

Addie felt the walls of her office shift and shrink around her.

In her haste to call him she hadn't considered how he might react. But now, hearing his voice, she felt confused and thwarted, for he sounded exactly as he always had: cool, smooth, in control. Almost as though the last five years had never happened.

She gritted her teeth. What had she expected? Anger? Outrage? That would mean being emotional, and Malachi King didn't *do* emotional.

Her hands felt suddenly hot and clammy and, closing her eyes, she gripped the phone more tightly. She might not like it, but the truth was that it would take more than hearing from his estranged wife to make Malachi lose his cool. After all, even when their marriage had been disintegrating he had been like the eye of the storm: calm, detached. Separate.

But that was all in the past now. This phone call wasn't about raking over their personal history. It was about her husband's despicable behaviour *now*. And its impact on children's futures. Breathing out, she opened her eyes.

'How can you even mention the word *honour* after

how you've acted? And don't act so surprised to hear from me. I sent you an email ten minutes ago—'

She broke off suddenly, anger making her trip over her words, the misery and pain suddenly as fresh as it had been five years ago. How could that be? It didn't seem fair to feel like that. But then she had never really got over his deception. Nothing—not even her job—had ever really filled the void that Malachi had left.

A shiver ran through her body and she was grateful that he couldn't see her face, see just how strongly he affected her. Her eyes narrowed. There was no way she was about to give him the satisfaction of hearing it in her voice either and, trying to project poise and confidence, she said coolly, 'I know you're short on empathy, Malachi, and that you have the morals of a shark, but I didn't think even *you* would stoop this low.'

The plane was turning. They were making their descent. Frowning, Malachi flipped open his laptop, punching the keyboard, his face impassive as he searched through his emails.

'I feel your pain, sweetheart,' he said softly, 'and I wish I could help. But unfortunately I'm a little baffled as to what it is you think I've done.'

Despite the neutrality of his words, he felt her anger gritty on his skin. Five years of silence and she randomly decided to ring up and shout at him about his morals and his lack of empathy. He frowned again. For some inexplicable reason she had once managed to turn his world upside down and inside out. It was a little surprising, not to say unsettling, to discover that she could still do so.

But his surprise was forgotten as finally he found the source of her outrage. So *that* was why she was so upset!

Leaning back, he stared at the screen, his eyes fixed on his wife's name. In theory, their conversation was over. He could and probably should simply hand the matter over to his social responsibilities department but—his eyes gleamed—where would be the fun in *that*?

'As I'm sure you remember, I run a huge operation,' he said disingenuously. 'Perhaps you could explain exactly what it is you *think* I've done.'

Addie felt a flash of impatience.

First he pulled the financial rug from under her feet, and now he was pretending he didn't know anything about it. She might have been idealistic and eager enough to take his words at face value when they'd first met, five years ago, but thanks to Malachi she'd become an expert in double-dealing.

'Oh, please! Do you *really* think I'm that stupid? You can't bluff your way out of this one, Malachi. This is not some game of cards!'

'Indeed it is not. Card games have rules, and players don't tend to screech unfounded accusations at one another.'

The taunting note in his voice made her heart bang in her throat, and suddenly she was gripping the phone so tightly her hand hurt.

'They are not unfounded. And I'm not screeching,' she snapped.

Damn him. He was so infuriating! Always twisting the facts. And so impossible to pin down. Unless she concentrated hard she was going to lose track of why she'd rung him in the first place, and probably end up saying or doing something stupid. Although not as stupid as agreeing to marry him.

Her blue eyes hardened like water turning to ice. Reining in her temper, she said crisply, 'You signed the letter, Malachi. I have it in front of me.'

'I sign lots of letters,' he said smoothly. 'It could be anything. Dry cleaning. Overdue library book.'

Addie gritted her teeth. She had rung him in anger, *knowing* that right was on her side. Only now he was making her fury seem out of place—comical, even— as though she was trying to rob a bank with a water pistol. Worse, she could feel herself responding to the teasing note in his voice.

It was suddenly hard to breathe. Memories of the past were pressing in on her. Memories of the man she had loved—not just because of his staggering good looks but because he was cool and funny. *And flirty.*

She felt her insides tighten and a prickling heat began to spread slowly over her skin.

Even the most prosaic of words sounded warm and honeyed when spoken in that slow, sexy drawl of his. For a moment she allowed herself to picture his handsome face, that wicked gleam in those dark, hypnotic eyes, the slight upward curve to his gorgeous lush mouth—

Her heart was banging.

Don't forget the lies that spilled from that gorgeous lush mouth, she reminded herself coldly.

Particularly those he'd told her at the altar. Next time she felt like reminiscing over her husband's charms she needed to remember those lies and how they'd left her struggling even to get out of bed some mornings.

Gripping the phone more tightly, she lifted her chin. 'As you well know it's about the centre. So quit pretending that you had nothing to do with stopping my funding.'

Staring at the screen in front of him, Malachi shifted slowly in his seat, waiting, thinking, deliberating.

Until two minutes ago her letter had just been one of the many that were handed to him every week. And yes, he'd signed it. But did she really believe he would do such a thing to her charity out of malice? His face tightened. Probably, and he knew she had reason to think so, but he didn't like the fact that she thought so badly of him.

'You're right. I did sign the letter,' he said coolly. 'But, like I said before, I sign hundreds of letters every week. I don't read them all—or even write them, actually. Except those that are personal.'

'You mean like a letter to your *wife*?' Addie said acidly.

Malachi stared straight ahead. Her words stung, as she'd intended them to.

'I suppose I asked for that.'

Feeling a stab of pain, Addie breathed out slowly. 'Yes. You did.'

At least if he'd known nothing about the letter she might have been able to believe he would have acted differently. But how had he not noticed her name? Or remembered her charity? For a moment she contemplated asking him, but her pride forbade her from revealing the grinding ache of misery in her chest. Besides, what was the point? It was all too long ago to matter.

She heard him sigh.

'I can understand how it might have looked to you. But it's quite simple, really. We offer financial support to emerging charities for a fixed period—in your case five years. By that time we would expect the project to be up and running and the funding would be cancelled. My signing the letter was just a formality.'

A formality!

Her lips twisted.

What a perfect footnote to a marriage that had been nothing more than a business strategy—for Malachi, at least.

'So,' he said softly, 'is that it? Are we good? Or is there something else you want to discuss?'

Her stomach gave a lurch as his words ricocheted inside her head. What did he mean? *Something else you want to discuss.* Was he just being polite? But even if a prickling tension *hadn't* begun to spread over her skin she knew he wasn't. She could hear the dare in his voice, the challenge, fluttering between them like a ribbon in a breeze.

Damn him. If Malachi wanted to talk about their relationship he could bring it up himself. Speaking to him had been a necessary evil. But she absolutely, definitely wasn't going to make polite conversation with him. And she certainly didn't want to discuss their marriage.

Or did she?

Her cheeks grew warm. Ringing Malachi had been a spur of the moment act. Confronted by what she'd seen as a deliberate act of provocation, she'd been swept along in a rush of anger and outrage. Only now her anger was slipping away, and reluctantly she found herself acknowledging the *whole* truth.

That she could simply have ignored the letter.

Or let a solicitor contact King Industries.

Or asked to speak to someone other than Malachi.

But she hadn't because deep down, buried beneath the resentment and the pain and the hurt, she had *wanted* that chance to speak to him. She shivered. It had been reckless, stupid. But surely she could forgive herself that one moment of weakness. After all, didn't every disappointed lover have some tiny sliver of longing to hold on to their fantasy of love?

But that didn't mean she was ready to discuss her failed marriage with the man who had trampled on that selfsame heart. Any more than she'd been willing five years ago to share more than the barest details about herself —particularly those concerning her life-changing accident. It would have required a trust that simply wasn't there.

She breathed in sharply. Right now, however, there were other less personal but more pressing matters to resolve. Like getting her funding back.

'No. We're *not* good! I accept that you didn't personally choose to stop the funding but that doesn't change the fact that it has stopped.'

She paused. Despite her bravado her heart had started to thump inside her chest. It had been easier when anger had been driving her. But ranting and raging was clearly not going to persuade Malachi to rethink his decision. That would require a softer, more conciliatory touch. Appalled, she licked her lips nervously. *Stay neutral and stick to the facts*, she told herself quickly. The funding was vital, the centre's work lasting and beneficial, and of course his generosity would be much appreciated. But, first off she needed to test the water.

Lifting her chin, she said firmly, 'Which is why I'd like you to change your mind.'

Malachi leaned back in his seat, a predatory smile curling his lip. It was a reasonable request. But it was still a request. One that *he* had the power to approve.

Or not.

'As I explained,' he said smoothly, 'I receive many requests for financial support. You yourself know of many deserving charities in Miami.'

'I do,' she agreed hurriedly. 'But the work we do with the children is enormously valuable and unique to the city.'

Standing up, Malachi stretched slowly and stifled a yawn. Could he be bothered to drag this conversation out any longer? The amount under discussion would barely make a dent in his billions. He could have a new agreement written up in minutes, sign it and say goodbye to Addie for ever. Or he could simply refuse to renew the funding and hand it over to his lawyers. Either way, in a matter of minutes she would be off the phone and out of his life for good.

His chest ached. Except now that she'd finally made contact with him saying goodbye was the last thing on his mind.

'True enough,' he said finally. 'But, be that as it may, there would have to be exceptional circumstances for me to renew your funding.'

The phone twitched in her hand and holding it suddenly felt dangerous, as though it had morphed into a snake. There was a long, pulsing silence and Addie licked her lips again. His words were innocuous enough, but she could feel the danger shimmering behind them. Only, having come this far, what choice did she have?

She took a deep breath. 'What kind of exceptional circumstances?'

Her voice sounded taut and high—too high. To her strained nerves it sounded desperate, needy—hardly the image she was striving to convey. As far as Malachi was concerned she wanted him to think that she was doing just fine. Better than fine, in fact. She wanted him to imagine her as gorgeous and successful—and utterly out of his reach.

Breathing in sharply, she glanced down at the letter on her desk and scowled. 'What kind of circumstances?' she repeated more steadily.

Malachi stared in silence out of the window. The

sun was turning the sky a pale gold. It was going to be another beautiful day. A small smile curled his lips.

'I don't know,' he said truthfully. 'But I imagine I would have to look into the case closely...' He paused, relishing the tension quivering down the phone line. '*Very* closely. In fact I would definitely have to meet with the applicant. In person.'

Addie held her breath. Her body seemed to have turned to liquid.

'N-No!' she stammered. 'I don't think that's a good idea.'

'But *I* do. I don't just hand out money to anyone, you know.'

'I'm not anyone!' she snapped. 'I'm your wife.'

Too late, she saw that she had fallen into his trap.

'Which is another good reason for us to meet,' he said slowly. 'We can talk about our marriage.'

Her office suddenly felt airless. Her nerves were shrieking like a car alarm. Suddenly he wanted to talk about their marriage? Was he mad? Or deluded?

'No, we can't! I won't. Dragging up the past isn't going to change anything,' she said shakily. 'We just have to accept it was a mistake—'

'Was it?'

Addie blinked. It had been a disaster. And Malachi knew that as well as she did.

'Yes. It was.' She spoke too quickly, the words keeping pace with her heartbeat. 'I can't imagine what I was thinking!'

'Can't you?'

She took a quick breath, almost like a gasp. His

voice was slow and glowing with a heat that she could feel down the phone. A heat that crept under her skin and coiled around her heart so that suddenly she couldn't seem to breathe properly.

'That's probably because what we shared had very little to do with thought, sweetheart.'

He paused and she felt the heat spike inside her.

'Mostly it had to do with tearing each other's clothes off.'

Addie swallowed. Her hand felt damp against the phone. A drumroll of fear and longing was beating so loudly that for a second she thought it was coming from outside of her body.

'I don't remember,' she whispered.

'I don't believe you,' he murmured. 'I know you remember that time in the lift.'

She shivered. She did remember. Could remember it as if she were there now, watching herself and Malachi, his hand slipping beneath her dress, her body arching against his as she tugged feverishly at his belt.

With a pure effort of will she dragged her mind back to the present.

'Apart from being irrelevant to this discussion, it was all a long time ago. So, no, I *don't*,' she lied. 'Unlike you, Malachi, my life, like most people's lives, does not just revolve around sex!'

'You think? Then you're either excessively naive or an extremely bad liar.'

She heard the amusement in his voice.

'Sex drives *all* human life. What did you think our relationship was based on? A mutual love of seafood!'

Addie felt a dull pain start to throb in her chest. No. She hadn't thought it was based on seafood. Fool that she was, she'd actually hoped and believed that their relationship had been based on love. An ache spread through her chest, hot and dark like a summer storm. Only love required honesty and trust, not secrets and lies. And neither of them had ever told the other the truth.

'I don't like seafood any more,' she snapped. 'Nor do I want to listen to your one-dimensional views on relationships. And I especially don't want to discuss them, or anything else for that matter, with you in person.'

'Really?' he said in that slow, sexy drawl that made her blood hum and her skin turn to glue. 'That's a shame. You see, I was hoping you'd meet me for lunch so we could discuss your funding. You *do* want me to renew your funding, don't you, sweetheart?'

Addie stood up, pushing her seat back with such force that it fell backwards onto the floor. But she barely noticed, such was her panic to block out that seductive velvet-smooth voice. And the urgent response of her body to it.

'I'm not going to meet you for lunch, Malachi!'

'You think dinner might be better?' he said disingenuously, completely ignoring the fury in her voice. 'I'm happy to do either. What do you fancy? French? Or what about some ceviche? There's a great new Peruvian place just opened up.'

Dinner! A vein was pulsing painfully in her forehead and mechanically she pressed her fingers against it. 'I don't want to eat French or Peruvian,' she said shrilly. 'And I'm not meeting you for lunch or dinner or any other kind of meal.'

'Pity!' His voice was dark and loaded. 'Because that's the only way you're going to get your funding out of me.'

'Fine,' she snarled. 'Then I'll just have to get the money some other way.'

'I'm sure you will,' he murmured. 'You always were very *imaginative*, as I recall.'

Her temper finally snapped. 'You are disgusting and I never want to speak to you again.'

He laughed. 'I'm a little unclear. Did we agree on lunch or dinner?'

With a howl of fury, she hung up.

Still laughing, Malachi switched off his phone and dropped it onto the desk. He gazed thoughtfully across the plane's cabin, wondering what she would wear when he saw her again. For, whatever she'd said, their meeting was as inevitable as the sun rising and setting. His heart began to thump; his blood was pumping, slow and heavy. Nor was it hate that had made her hang up on him. It was fear. She was scared—scared of the connection between them and her response to it.

And so she should be.

His grey eyes flared and feeling his groin harden, he let out a long, slow breath as a trickle of anticipation ran down his spine.

She might not have been the perfect wife he'd imagined, but Addie had never been boring. On the contrary—she had been feisty and stubborn and impulsive. Which meant that lunch—or, better still, dinner—was a fore-gone conclusion. All that remained was for him to choose a restaurant and a tie.

And, letting out a sigh of satisfaction, he settled back into his chair to enjoy the view.

CHAPTER TWO

'No. I QUITE UNDERSTAND.' Trying her hardest to keep the note of disappointment out of her voice, Addie picked up her pen and drew a line firmly through the last name on the list in her notepad. 'And thank you for giving me so much of your time.'

Flipping open her laptop, she scrolled slowly through the column of figures on the screen. Finally she let out a long, slow breath. It was hopeless. Despite all her efforts she had barely enough funds to cover next month's rent and a few utility bills. Even if she added in her meagre savings she certainly couldn't afford to pay her staff's salaries.

Leaning back in her chair, she bit her lip. If she told them what had happened she knew they would offer to forego their pay. But why should they? she thought angrily. Why should they suffer because she had let her arrogant, maddening ex get under her skin?

Her head was pounding. And it wasn't just because of her precarious finances. Speaking to Malachi again had stirred up feelings she had buried deep, deep down, and now she was battling emotions she still wasn't ready to acknowledge or resolve.

Her heart gave a lurch. It wasn't only her feelings she couldn't face. She'd spent the last five years more or less pretending that her marriage had never happened. Now, in the space of twenty-four hours, she'd been forced to confront not only her husband but the state of estrangement between them.

Sighing, she slumped back in her seat and reluctantly contemplated the mess she'd made of her private life. Since splitting with Malachi she'd focused her energies on work. Yes, she'd been on a few 'dates' but no man ever quite measured up to him. But then she hadn't just fallen for Malachi. She'd dived in headfirst, captivated not only by his looks and charm but by how he'd made her feel like her true self. The self she'd discovered through music and lost the night of her accident. Only through music had she felt able to be the real Addie—wild and free. And Malachi had made her feel like that too.

But not for long. Pretty soon she'd been out of her depth and drowning. Only by that time she'd become his wife.

Her pulse twitched and she shifted in her seat. It had all happened so long ago. So why were they still married?

As far as Malachi was concerned it was probably because he'd forgotten all about her until yesterday, when she'd called him, whereas she— Her face coloured painfully. She was still married because she was a coward. The thought of seeing him again had been just too painful. In the months following their separation she had vowed to confront him and demand a divorce, but she had always found a reason not to do so. And so the months had become years.

Five long years. In fact, tomorrow it would be five years exactly.

Remembering her wedding day—his tension, her confusion over his parents' absence—she felt a shiver of sadness. It was obvious even then that what they'd shared was nothing more than physical attraction.

She frowned. But her marriage wasn't the issue here.

She needed money, fast, and if having lunch with Malachi meant that she got her funding then maybe she should just call him. No doubt he was sitting there in his office, smugly waiting for her to do just that. But she sure as hell wasn't going to help him choose a restaurant as if it was some kind of a date. Her eyes narrowed. She needed to do something to make it clear that she was meeting him on her own terms.

So why not surprise him at lunch? All she would have to do was follow him to wherever he was eating and confront him, and then finally she might wipe the self-satisfied smile from that gorgeous mouth of his. Easy!

Her breath jammed in her throat.

Easy?

One look from Malachi had once been enough to turn her into a rippling mass of desire. But not any more, she told herself firmly. For even if her body hadn't learned the consequences of falling for that

shimmering, sensual gaze her mind had, she had more
sense and pride than to let it happen again.

Was it only lunchtime?

His grey eyes widening with disbelief, Malachi
glanced at the one-of-a-kind Swiss-made watch on
his wrist. Unusually for him, the day had seemed to
drag—and his mind was only half on work. The other
half was picking over his conversation with Addie.

Leaning back, he smiled slowly, remembering the
frustration in her voice.

She'd been good and riled. But it wasn't only exasperation that had made her so hot and bothered. He'd
heard another kind of heat.

And just like that an image of Addie flared inside
his brain. The soft pouting lips, glossy red curls and
legs like a thoroughbred in the Kentucky Derby. All
wrapped up in a take-it-or-leave-it manner that he'd
had no choice but to take…

Breathing heavily, he shifted in his seat, remembering the feverish touch of her mouth against his, the heat
between them blurring their edges so that it had been
impossible to feel where she'd ended and he'd begun.

He smiled grimly. For most of his life he'd watched
his mother and father use passion and emotion like
poker dice, uncaring of the consequences. As an adult,
away from their orbit, he'd sworn never to follow in
their footsteps. *His* private life would be conducted in
the realm of reason.

*Only then he'd met Addie, and thrown away caution
and control and broken every damn rule in the book.*

A pulse began to beat in his neck and suddenly his chair felt cramped, confined. Standing up, he walked quickly across his office to the large floor-to-ceiling window that overlooked the gaming area of his flagship Miami casino. He breathed in sharply. There were nearly seven hundred gaming tables down there, not including the *club privé*, each one offering a change of fortune, a new beginning, a better life.

Watching people as they gave everything they had—sometimes literally—to the turn of a card or the roll of a dice seemed to him to represent the rawest, most pure expression of what it meant to be human. It was all there—hope and hunger, fear, and the desire to win. He found it fascinating, stimulating. But not as fascinating or stimulating as the thought of seeing his estranged wife again.

Staring down at the men and women, their faces tight with concentration, he felt a flicker of anticipation. She'd told him she never wanted to speak to him again. But she would. She'd have no choice. And not just because of the money.

His eyes gleamed.

So, where should he take her for lunch?

Snatching his jacket from the back of his chair, he tugged it on. Addie would no doubt refuse to meet him if there was even a hint that they would be alone together. A busy, open-plan restaurant would be better. His eyes gleamed again. He knew just the place.

Opening his door, he was met by the startled faces of his secretary, Chrissie, and her assistant.

'I'm going out for lunch.'

'But—'

The women glanced up at him in confusion.

'You're meeting Andy here at twelve-thirty,' said Chrissie. 'You always meet him.'

It was true. Most days he met his casino managers as they came on shift. But today was different.

'So it'll be a nice change for both of us,' he said smoothly. 'Call Eights. My usual table. And tell Andy I'm indisposed.'

'Would you like your car to be brought round to the front, sir?'

Malachi shook his head and smiled. 'No, thank you, Chrissie. I need a bit of fresh air.'

He ran a finger under his collar. After thinking about Addie, what he actually needed was a cold shower, but a tall chilled mojito might just be a tolerable alternative!

The restaurant was crowded with the usual mix of suave businessmen and glamorous, golden-limbed women. His table was set slightly apart from the other diners, with a view over the ocean. Like all the best views in the world, it was unchanging and yet never the same.

His choices made, he waved away the waiters and sat back, his eye drawn to the horizon between sea and sky, where dense black clouds hovered above the turquoise water. A storm was coming. According to the weather reports, it was due to hit land just after three. Not that he minded. A storm—bad weather in general—was good for business. But it meant that his lunch might have to be slightly curtailed.

His phone gave a small shudder and, turning, he glanced at it, his face expressionless. It was a message from Henry, asking him to call. But he didn't want his father's voice inside his head. Not when his mind was filled with thoughts of Addie.

He picked up his glass. The wine was an interesting choice, the crisp hint of apple surprising him. But it wasn't the wine that caused him to put down his glass. It was the woman walking through the restaurant towards him.

Like every other man in the room, he watched her intently as she wove sinuously between the tables. He felt a rush of excitement. *The weathermen had been wrong.* The storm had already hit town. And her name was Hurricane Addie!

Staring defiantly ahead, Addie made her way across the room. Walking into the restaurant, she'd felt a fluttering panic. It was one thing deciding in anger to gatecrash his lunch and cajole him into renewing her funding—quite another to confront him in cold blood. In theory, she could tell herself that she no longer cared about him and that he was just another businessman on her list. She could even remind herself that he was the man who had lied to her face and broken her heart. But all that reason and logic had been forgotten when she'd pulled open the door and stepped into the restaurant.

Despite the fact that the room was packed with diners, she spotted him in a heartbeat. No one but Malachi had that invisible but tangible push-me-pull-me energy. Radiating out from him like rays from the sun, it tugged her gaze across the room to where he sat, gazing out at the ocean like some buccaneer on the high seas. She breathed in sharply, her hand rising involuntarily, protectively in front of her, as though to ward off the full intensity of his masculinity.

He was even more beautiful than she remembered, with his dark hair falling across his forehead, that sculpted poet's profile and those eyes…the grey shifting and darkening like a constantly changing winter sky. He looked cool and relaxed in a tailored charcoal-grey suit that was a shade lighter than his eyes—and worth every cent of the billions of dollars he was rumoured to have made from his gaming empire.

Her head was spinning; the noise of the room sounded distant and distorted. But even though it was clear he still had the power to throw her off balance, she damn well wasn't going to reveal that fact to Malachi.

Her hands curling into fists, she walked purposefully towards him and stopped in front of his table. Her back felt as if it was burning beneath the combined female envy in the room, but her blue gaze was cool and scornful as they stared at one another in silence.

It was she who spoke first. 'You wanted to have lunch with me.' Her voice was husky, her cheeks flushed with colour. 'So here I am.'

'Yes, you are,' he said softly. He stared in undisguised appreciation at the clinging black dress. Or rather at the swelling curves beneath the fabric. 'You look incredible, sweetheart. Life must be treating you well. I feel like I should be the one asking *you* for money.'

Addie lifted her chin. 'Who knows? Maybe one day

you will be.' She rested one slim hand on her hip. 'So, are you going to ask me to sit down? Or have you changed your mind?'

'In that dress? Not a chance. Come and join me.' Patting the seat beside him, he grinned as, ignoring his gesture, Addie sat down on the opposite side of the table.

As though her arrival had triggered some hidden switch, not one but two waiters immediately appeared beside them, and her shoulders lowered with relief as the daunting prospect of being on her own with him was temporarily postponed. But her reprieve couldn't last for ever and finally they were alone.

'I just want to make it clear that *I'm* paying,' she said quickly. Their eyes met—hers the same, rebellious blue as a teenage tattoo, his glinting, grey. 'It's only fair.'

His gaze fixed on her face and he stared at her thoughtfully, then shrugged. 'Fine. You can buy me lunch. But I warn you, I'm not a cheap date.'

Addie stilled. 'This is not a *date*, Malachi. And that kind of remark is why I'm buying lunch. So there aren't any mixed messages.'

He grinned. 'You know me, sweetheart. The only thing I like mixed are my cocktails. Speaking of which—at least let me buy you a drink. Do you still like Bellinis?'

She swallowed, feeling a stabbing within. And then a softness. 'You remembered…'

His eyes never left her face. 'Of course. I remember everything about you and our time together.'

The softness hardened and she shivered inside. Was

that what their marriage had been to him? A portion of hours and days? Her heart began to beat faster.

'Good!' She swallowed. 'Then you'll remember how important my charity is to the children it helps. And, no, thank you. I don't want a Bellini.'

He waved a hand across the table at her negligently.

'Some wine, then? Or is my presence intoxicating enough for you?'

Tucking her legs beneath the table, Addie forced herself to meet his cool grey gaze. 'I don't drink at business meetings.' she said primly.

'Neither do I,' agreed Malachi, lifting the glass of wine to his lips. 'It's very unprofessional. But fortunately I don't class our meeting as anything other than a cause for celebration.'

She stared at him blankly. 'Celebration! I don't know what you're talking about.'

'Of course you do.' Beneath the restaurant's lights his eyes looked lighter, almost silver. 'It was you who reminded me.' He held out his glass and tapped it against her tumbler of water. 'Happy Anniversary, sweetheart!'

Addie felt her skin grow cold. His eyes were glittering with an emotion she didn't fully understand and, quickly turning her head, she fixed her gaze on the view of the ocean just as their meals arrived.

The food was both delicious and beautifully presented, but Addie found it impossible to enjoy her lobster salad.

'Even if it is our anniversary,' she said coldly, 'I hardly think that's relevant to today's discussion. Personally I'd be happier if we just stuck to the *real* reason why we're both here.'

'Of course,' he murmured. 'If it makes you more comfortable.'

Addie glowered at him. Comfortable! As if!

The only reason she was still sitting there was the children and her colleagues. Otherwise, had she not chosen to wear such ridiculously high heels, she would happily have turned round and run as fast as possible from that deceptively guileless face.

But breathing out slowly, she pressed her nails into the palms of her hands. At least she looked the part. Even if it had meant selling her bike. The important thing was that while she might need his help, *he didn't need to know that*. She looked cool and classy and in control. Not like a woman looking for a favour.

Now all she had to do was stay focused. But, glancing across the table, she felt a pulse leap in her throat as she looked up into his glittering grey gaze.

'You're very quiet, sweetheart. I thought you wanted to talk?' Lolling back against the leather upholstery, Malachi gazed at her intently.

She shrugged. 'I was just thinking.'

'Then I should probably be leaving!' His eyes, light and dancing, fixed on her face even as the corners of his mouth began to tilt upwards. 'A quiet woman is like a hand grenade. A quiet woman *thinking* is like a hand grenade with the pin pulled out.'

His curving smile waited for her reply and she licked her lips, her heart fluttering beneath his scrutiny.

And then, just in time, she remembered that there was an actual reason for her being there—other than just to gawp at Malachi's cheekbones. Feeling clumsy, hoping he didn't suspect the reason for her distracted behaviour, she pulled out a folded piece of paper from her bag and handed it to him.

'That's the original agreement.'

He took it and opened it. His face was impassive as he scanned the contents. Finally he looked up at her. 'It's strange, don't you think? The two of us? Together again?'

She'd been expecting him to refer to the letter. Instead, caught off guard, she had to force down the tangled mass of emotion that reared up inside her in response both to his words and the probing focus of his eyes.

'Th-there is no "two of us",' she said shakily. Her eyes darted away from him and round the room, seeking something solid and reassuring. Fixing on two burly businessmen at the bar, she felt her shoulders relax slightly. 'And we're not together.'

He smiled slowly. 'Then why are you scared?'

Her temper flared. 'I'm not scared.' She hesitated. 'Just a little apprehensive, I suppose.' She met his gaze defiantly.

'Would it help if I promised not to drop my napkin?' he said softly.

A warm tide swept over her skin, as hot and strong as a hurricane. But no hurricane could ever be as devastating or dangerous as Malachi King, she thought wildly. Her cheeks burning, she fixed her eye on the smooth white linen tablecloth. But she could feel his eyes, dark and implacable as granite, seeking her out.

'I'd rather you didn't bring *that* up now.' Her skin felt as if it was on fire; her heartbeat felt so loud she was surprised the other diners hadn't stopped eating to stare at her.

'When *would* you like me to bring it up?' he asked smoothly.

'N-never!' Her voice was trembling and she shook her head. 'It's just not appropriate!'

He shrugged, his face dispassionate. 'I don't remember you complaining at the time.'

His eyes were like the shimmering headlights of a car. She stared at him helplessly, hypnotised, horrified by her body's fierce, swift response to his words and the image they conjured up.

Had she *really* let him do that to her? In a *restaurant*? There was an ache low down in her pelvis. Her whole body was suddenly shaking and it felt as though her insides were being sucked into a whirlpool. A memory—perfect, impossible, spinning apart into a hundred shades of gold—slid into her head. It had been so wildly, shockingly exciting. Even now she could hardly believe it had happened. Or that she had let it. What had she been *thinking*?

She felt her chest tighten and her skin start to burn, for of course Malachi had been right. What they'd shared had had very little to do with thought. Their entire relationship had been founded on passion, in his arms she'd been fierce, wild, hungry for his touch; he had awoken the hot, sensual woman beneath the quiet, dutiful young pianist who'd practised her scales every day—

Her stomach dipped. But thanks to him that woman didn't exist any more.

Meeting his gaze, she gave him an icy stare. 'Do you want me to leave right now?'

His eyes flickered across her face and, reaching out, he picked up a piece of bread and bit into it with strong white teeth. 'Wouldn't that be a little premature? I thought you came here to discuss your funding? If you leave now, sweetheart, you'll go empty-handed. Besides…'

He gave her a slow, sexy grin that made something hot and scratchy scrape inside her.

'I'm sure you don't want to miss dessert.'

He was calling her bluff. He knew she had no choice but to stay. Meeting his gaze, her eyes narrowed into sharp shards of blue. He was so smug and annoying. How she hated him!

Except that she didn't.

Not unless that ball of hot liquid heat swelling inside her so that her ribs ached was how hatred felt.

She swallowed. Around her she could almost hear the air hissing when it came into contact with her over-heated skin. Surely she wasn't supposed to feel like this—so breathless, so dazzled.

Watching him lounge back against the leather, his eyes gleaming with undisguised satisfaction, she felt a rush of pure white anger. 'I know what you're doing,' she said breathlessly. 'You're trying to make me lose my temper so that I'll leave.'

He raised his eyebrows. 'Is that right? You know, it never ceases to amaze me how women can misinterpret even the simplest statement and put some spin on it.'

'Spin!' It took every ounce of willpower she had not to throw the contents of her glass into his infuriatingly handsome face. 'You making vile innuendos is not spin,' she snapped.

'I didn't make any innuendos. I was merely recounting historical fact.'

His eyes were dancing with a malice that made her want to scream out loud. He was impossible. And this meeting was a farce.

'Well, I didn't come here to have a history lesson,' she hissed. 'Especially a highly selective and one-sided one.'

The waiter was back again. 'Was everything to your satisfaction, Mr King?'

'It was perfect, thank you. The scallops were sublime and my wife thoroughly enjoyed her lobster salad—didn't you, darling?'

My wife!

Startled, her eyes met his. 'Yes, I did.' Glancing up, she gave the waiter a perfunctory smile. 'It was delicious.' She waited, fuming, until the plates had been cleared away and they were alone again. 'Why did you call me that?'

His look of blank incomprehension made her want to throttle him with her napkin.

'Why wouldn't I call you that? That is what you are,' he said smoothly. 'Surely you didn't think you could

just waltz back into my life and start demanding money
but somehow avoid discussing our marriage?'

She shivered as his gaze fixed on her bare ring finger but, refusing to be cowed, she drew back her shoulders and met his stare defiantly.

'I don't want to talk about our marriage.'

'Clearly,' he said softly. 'If you had, you would have
got in touch over the last five years.'

She felt the blood drain from her face. 'There was
nothing stopping *you* from getting in touch. And I
didn't waltz back into your life and demand anything.
I'm here because you *insisted* that I meet you and now
you want to *dictate* what we talk about.'

Her voice echoed round the room and, looking up,
she froze. The restaurant was no longer packed with
diners. In fact she and Malachi appeared to be the
only two people remaining, apart from the businessmen at the bar. She watched, her stomach clenching,
as a waiter discreetly cleared a table and left the room.

'We need to leave,' she said hurriedly, glancing
round again. 'Lunchtime service is clearly over.'

Glancing over his shoulder, Malachi shrugged.
'They can wait.'

Her eyes narrowed. 'You are *so* arrogant. These people have lives, Malachi. You can't just expect them to
hang around for hours.'

'Why not? That's what they're paid to do,' he said
casually.

She glowered at him. 'But not by you.'

There was a sudden, stinging pause. Glancing up,

she saw that he was surveying her steadily, an odd light
in his eyes. And suddenly the penny dropped.

'You own this place?' she croaked.

He nodded slowly, enjoying her shock. 'Yes, I do.'
He paused, and there was a courteous edge to his voice
that disguised the brutality of his words. 'That's why
I chose to meet you here.'

She stared at him in confusion. For a moment her
mind simply couldn't absorb his words. 'But you didn't
choose to meet me,' she said slowly. 'I followed you
here.'

He looked at her almost regretfully, and suddenly
her heart was beating so fast she thought it would burst.
Glancing over at the men at the bar, she felt her jawline
tighten. Had she *really* thought they were businessmen?

She shook her head in disbelief at her own naivety.
'You had me followed. By them.'

Their eyes met—hers wide with outrage, his shimmering with satisfaction and her hands balled into fists.
He was enjoying himself, the bastard!

He shrugged. 'It's their job. They spotted you outside the office.'

Heat was blistering her skin. He'd played her—acting
as if he was surprised when all along he'd known she
was coming. She felt a spasm of nausea. But was it that
surprising, really? He'd always been good at pretending.
Look at the way he'd convinced her that he loved her.

She stood up so suddenly that the men at the bar
leaped off their stools.

'I should never have come here. As if you could *ever*
behave like a mature, responsible adult—'

'Sit down.' Leaning forward, he spoke quietly, but the authority in his voice was enough to make her stop and look at him.

'Why? I don't want to talk to you.'

'Yes, you do. That's why you followed me.'

He leaned back in his seat, unfazed by her anger, and irritably she realised that despite her plans he was the one calling the shots. He always had been. It was just that she hadn't realised it until that moment.

'Come on, Addie. Sit down.' His voice had shifted, softened. 'Look, I'm going to give you your money. I always was.' Reaching into his jacket, he pulled out a piece of paper and slid it across the table. 'It's a copy of a bank transaction. It was wired to your account...' he glanced casually at his watch '...about twenty minutes ago.' His eyes flickered over her taut expression. 'Relax, sweetheart. You got what you came for. That *is* what you came for, isn't it?' He smiled. 'Now, why don't you just take a seat and we can both try and act like *mature, responsible adults.*'

Trying to keep what little remained of her dignity, she sat down and stared at him coldly.

His eyes gleamed. 'Go on. Take it.'

Reluctantly she reached out and picked up the slip of paper. Staring down at it, she felt her face drain of colour. 'This is the wrong amount.' She looked back down, then, blinking, lifted her head in confusion. 'This is double what I was expecting.'

His eyes didn't leave hers. 'Think of it as an anniversary present.'

Carefully she put the paper down on the table. 'That's incredibly generous of you,' she said hoarsely.

'I'm glad you approve.'

His tone was pleasant, but something in his eyes made a shiver of apprehension run down her spine and she glanced nervously at the slip of paper again, half feaing she might have imagined it. But it was definitely real.

'It really is very generous,' she said stiffly. 'I don't know what I'd have done if I hadn't got the money. It means so much to me. Thank you.' She breathed out. 'How long will it take to clear?' She knew she sounded gauche but she didn't care. If Malachi wanted to gloat—let him.

'Around two hours.' He paused and looked past her at the dark clouds and the grey swelling sea outside, and she felt that shiver of apprehension spike painfully through her skin. 'But before you start spending it I need to make a few things clear.'

She nodded. 'Of course. Do you want me to sign a contract? I can do that now.'

He turned and slowly, very slowly, smiled at her.

'That won't be necessary. You see, that money didn't come from King Industries. It came from me. From my *personal* bank account. And my terms are *personal* too.'

She swallowed—or tried to swallow at least—past the lump in her throat.

'What do you mean "personal"?' she croaked. Around her the air felt hot and leaden and the room was growing darker. 'What do you *mean*?' she repeated, and the lump felt sharp and jagged now.

His voice was soft, just as it had been when he'd promised to love and honour and cherish her for ever. But the lines of his face were knife sharp and harder than stone.

'I've been very patient, sweetheart, but you owe me a honeymoon.'

'I—I don't understand.'

His gaze swept over her slowly.

'Then let me explain. I want you to come away with me for a month. To be my mistress.'

His eyes locked on to hers, pinning her against the leather upholstery.

'Do that and you can keep the money. Who knows? There might even be a little bonus in it for you as well.'

CHAPTER THREE

THERE WAS A LONG, pulsing silence. Across the table, Addie stared at him in mute disbelief, unable to believe what she had just heard. Slowly she picked over his words inside her head, turning and twisting them like pieces in a jigsaw puzzle, trying to make a different meaning. But each time the picture was the same.

His *mistress*!

The word sounded even harsher inside her head than when he'd spoken it out loud and her breath snarled in her throat. Maybe she had misunderstood him. Or maybe he was joking. But as she stole a glance at his cool, implacable face she realised with a jolt of fear that he was making a serious suggestion.

'Are you out of your mind?' she said shakily.

She stared down at the slip of paper, still lying on the table between them, clenching and unclenching her hands in her lap.

He shrugged, his cool gaze boring into her. 'Everything in life has a price, sweetheart.'

'A *price*! What are you talking about, Malachi? You just offered me money for sex!'

His gaze drifted lazily over her pale, stunned face. 'How very unromantic of you. I thought I was offering you the honeymoon we never had.'

She was suddenly hot with rage. 'Oh, please! You know exactly what you just said and it had nothing whatsoever to do with romance!'

Her words were tumbling from her lips so fast that she choked. As he gently pushed her glass of water towards her, she shoved his hand angrily away.

'I don't want any. I don't want anything from you.'

Stretching one muscular arm along the back of the banquette, he shook his head slowly. 'Now, we both know that's not true. Or are you saying that you want me to cancel that transfer into your account?'

Addie hesitated. She badly wanted to throw the money back in his face, but how could she? Without it the charity would struggle to pay the rent, let alone support the children. And she would lose a part of herself— the part she was most afraid to lose because it absorbed so much of the energy and emotion she had once given to performing. Once given to Malachi. Only she wasn't about to share that fact with him now.

Gritting her teeth, she lifted her eyes to his and he smiled slowly.

'See? Everything *does* have a price, sweetheart.'

He paused. His grey eyes watched her face with a satisfaction that made her want to scream.

'Besides, it's nothing you haven't done before.' His mouth curved, his grey eyes glittering provocatively.

She glared at him, her own blue eyes snapping fire. 'What? Sleep with a man for money?'

A muscle flickered in his cheek. 'I'm simply asking you to resume our relationship.'

'You are not! You're taking advantage of me.'

'No, I'm trying to negotiate a deal with you.'

'A *deal*? This isn't a deal. It's blackmail. And it's insulting—' Shaking her head, she pushed the slip of paper jerkily across the table towards him. 'I'm not some *escort* you pay by the day, Malachi! I'm your wife!'

'So *now* you want to talk about our marriage?'

His eyes held hers, so dark and dispassionate that suddenly she was frantic to leave. His crude proposal was bad enough. But she couldn't bear the thought of the two of them turning everything they'd once shared into something so twisted and ugly.

'No, I don't,' she said flatly. 'I don't want to talk to you about anything. In fact I've got a new deal for you. How about you keep your money? And I'll keep my pride.' Rising to her feet, she jerked her bag from the seat and glowered at him. 'Enjoy your honeymoon.'

'Addie—'

He was on his feet, reaching out for her. But, slipping away from his outstretched arm, she ran lightly across the restaurant and past the bodyguards. Yanking open the door, she stepped out into the street, her brain registering the black overcast sky just as a strong flurry of wind slammed against her.

Gasping, she tugged her thin jacket more tightly around her body and began to hurry down the rapidly emptying road. Her stormy encounter with Malachi had completely distracted her from the tempest raging outside, but now she realised that, like their relationship, the weather seemed to have taken a turn for the worse. Much worse!

She would have to get a cab, she thought despairingly as she glanced up at the swirling dark clouds. If she waited for a bus she'd be soaked.

Holding out her hand, she began to walk as quickly as her heels would allow, glancing back over her shoulder with increasing urgency until finally, hearing a car slow behind her, she turned with relief.

Only it wasn't a taxi. Her feet seemed to falter beneath her as a sleek black limousine complete with uniformed chauffeur drew up alongside her.

Her heart lurched and she took a hurried step backwards as one of the bodyguards from the restaurant leaped out from the passenger side. For a moment she thought he might grab her, but instead, turning swiftly, he opened the rear door and she felt her bones turn to ice as Malachi stepped out onto the pavement.

Turning cold blue eyes on him, she breathed out sharply as another gust of wind slapped into her. 'Shouldn't you be packing?' she snapped.

'Addie, please. Do you really want to be doing this now? Here?' He flinched as a gust of wind sent a newspaper flapping past his head. 'It's been downgraded, but this is still a big storm. We need to get out of it.'

'I know that. That's why I'm getting a cab. And there is no *"we"*.'

She glanced away down the deserted street.

'There are no cabs.' Malachi stepped in front of her,

his narrowed eyes at odds with the reasonable note in his voice. 'And it's getting pretty bad out here.'

As if to attest to the truth of his words, the first fat drops of water hit her face just as he reached out and touched her hand lightly.

'Let me give you a lift home, okay?'

Despite the chill of the rain, she felt heat explode inside her. The noise of the wind felt suddenly muffled, drowned out by the heavy thud of her heartbeat. But jerking her hand away, she gripped her jacket more tightly. It would have to be a Category 5 hurricane before she'd even *consider* getting into that car with him.

'I thought I made myself clear back at the restaurant.' She was having to shout now, against the buffeting breeze. 'I don't need anything from you, Malachi. So if you don't mind—'

'But I do. What if something happens to you? Imagine how that would look—'

Addie stared at him in disbelief, trying to banish the sharp stab of pain as his words dug into her brain. 'So this isn't about me and my safety. It's about you and your stupid image?'

For a moment she wanted to hurt him as he had hurt her. Was still hurting her. She clutched her bag against her chest, holding it in front of her like a shield as his eyes locked on to hers.

'I am worried about your safety.'

'So am I,' she snapped. 'Which is why I'm not getting in that car with you.'

All at once she was conscious of the calm surrounding him—as though his broad body was somehow absorbing the turbulence of the wind.

'Your choice, sweetheart. The back seat.' He smiled. 'Or the boot.'

Her hand tightened on the fabric of her jacket. 'Really! The *boot*? First you try and blackmail me—now you want to kidnap me!'

She watched the muscles in his arms swell against his beautifully tailored suit and instantly regretted her words. Knowing Malachi, he would have absolutely no qualms about tossing her into the boot of his car and, glancing down the street one last time, she made up her mind.

'Fine,' she said, through gritted teeth. 'You can give me a lift.'

His eyes glittered with what looked to her horribly like triumph and, willing herself to hold her temper in check, she edged past him. 'But just so you know—this doesn't change anything.'

Fuming, she slid along the leather as far as possible until she was pressed against the frame of the door. Already she was regretting her acquiescence, for despite the warmth and sanctuary of the car her nerves were singing, her body painfully alert at the realisation that she was about to be alone and up close with Malachi. It was asking for trouble.

But it was also too late to change her mind.

As he got in beside her she breathed out slowly, her eyes narrowing as he calmly gave her address to the chauffeur.

'Are you shivering or quivering?'

His voice broke into her thoughts and, turning, she scowled at him.

'Why do you care?'

'I was going to offer you my jacket.'

Her heart seemed to dissolve in her chest and a shivering heat crawled over her skin. 'Well, I'm not cold,' she said shortly. 'So you don't need to worry.'

'In that case you must be quivering.' He smiled. 'Dare I hope that it has anything to do with me?'

She knew he was teasing her but that didn't stop the sense of nervous unease she felt at his words. The sense that, despite her efforts to be poised and in control, she was making it transparently clear that her body still responded to him as it had always done.

Ignoring the burning in her cheeks, she lifted her chin. 'I'm sorry to disappoint you, Malachi, but it's been a long time since I was susceptible to your charms,' she said bitingly.

He tilted his head, his eyes skimming over her skin, sending ripples of heat in overlapping circles so that she was suddenly struggling to swallow.

'It's okay to admit it, sweetheart,' he said softly. 'I know you want me as desperately as I want you.'

Shoulders stiffening, she glared at him. Had he already forgotten his despicable and offensive proposal that she be his mistress? Probably. But knowing Malachi, he thought it was a perfectly reasonable suggestion. She knew from painful personal experience that he was happy to exploit everything and everyone— even…especially…his own wife—for his own ends.

Five years ago he'd used her image. Now he wanted to use her body.

The thought made her skin smart as though he'd slapped her.

'Don't flatter yourself. Right now I'm just desperate to get out of this car and away from you.'

Tipping his head back, Malachi laughed.

'Sorry, sweetheart, but you're stuck with me.'

'Only for as long as it takes your driver to get me home,' she snapped.

There was a short, pulsing silence, and through the rawness of her nerves she felt a drop of quicksilver shoot up her spine as he stared at her assessingly.

'We'll see.'

Her body was suddenly stiff and hollow and she felt a crack of fear open inside her.

'No, we will not! This is a one-off, Malachi.'

He shrugged, the muscles in his shoulders shifting against the fabric of his jacket.

'I see it more as a starting point.'

She shook her head slowly, her stomach lurching.

'For what? You paying me for sex.' Anger was flaring inside her once more.

'I just thought we could talk.'

'Look, Malachi, just because I accepted a lift from you, it doesn't mean I want to talk to you.' Fury rose up inside her. He was *so* insensitive. 'Why *would* I? After what you said in the restaurant?' She shook her head, the memory of his words making her hands ball in her lap. 'You insulted me!'

He stared at her in silence. It had been a spur-of-the-moment thing, asking her to be his mistress. Watching her walk towards him, the sight of her gorgeous body pressing against his eyeballs like a hot knife against butter, he'd made up his mind: he had to have her.

From nowhere, the idea had popped into his head, fully formed. But even now he wasn't completely sure why he'd actually gone ahead and suggested it to her.

Shifting in his seat, he gritted his teeth. Of course lust had obviously played a part. But there was more to his decision than just simple biology. When Addie had pitched into his life five years ago he'd seen her as an opportunity, a chance to have what he'd previously discounted as untenable, impossible. Before meeting her he'd never even wanted a wife—only she had been like an itch that wouldn't stop.

And then, realising how good she was for his image, it had been easy to persuade himself that she would make the perfect wife, her role in the local charity sector the yin to his yang as a ruthless, self-serving entrepreneur. Crucially, their partnership would help ensure a more positive reception for his new casino in downtown Miami.

His face stilled. But in the space of six months she'd turned his life inside out: she'd taken his heart and his name and discarded both. Worse, his failed marriage had unleashed a sense of disquiet and doubt that he'd never quite managed to shift, and her defection had left him smarting.

Now seeing her again, his body was aching with feverish sexual frustration. Persuading her to be his mistress had felt like the perfect solution, for it would solve his hunger *and* erase the feeling of powerlessness that was the legacy of their doomed relationship.

His mouth twisted. It was a feeling he loathed more than any other. A grim, painful reminder of a childhood dominated by the dark chaos of his parents' lives. Addie had seemed like the perfect riposte to their world. Bright, smart, independent—and sexy, of course. Only despite that he'd given her his name, and access to a world of wealth and power, she'd turned out to be just as needy as his parents, only instead of disorder, she brought doubts and accusations.

Remembering how it had felt when she'd left him— the shock, the humiliation—his mouth tightened. It was a bitter reminder of what happened when he let lust not logic make his decisions. But it wasn't too late; he could still walk away. Only walking away would feel like cashing in his chips. His eyes narrowed. Besides, her impassioned refusal had simply sharpened his determination to change her mind.

Only it wasn't going quite as smoothly as he would like…

He breathed out slowly. 'I want you, Addie, and I'm willing to pay to have you.'

Their eyes met and heat crawled over the skin at the back of her neck. She should have been outraged, and part of her was, for his statement was shocking in its almost carnal brutality. Only she couldn't deny that another, greater part was trembling with raw, feverish longing.

It didn't seem to matter that she was no longer in

love with him. He could still make her hands shake and her head spin.

She lifted her chin. *So could a waltzer at a funfair!* The difference was that when the ride ended, her heart and her pride would still be intact.

Gritting her teeth, she conjured up a memory of herself, face puffy with crying, slumped on her sofa beneath a duvet. *Remember that*, she told herself sternly. No amount of money or sexual gratification was worth those consequences.

Digging her fingernails into the palms of her hands, she raised her chin. 'But you can't have me, Malachi!'

She turned and glanced out of the window.

'This probably wasn't the best idea, so thank you for the lift but perhaps it might be better if you dropped me off here,' she said stiffly. 'I can look after myself.'

Malachi met her gaze. 'Is that why you're sitting all that way over there on your own?'

Watching her bite into her soft lower lip, he felt his groin harden. He could see the conflict in her eyes, could almost feel the nervous jolt of her pulse. She wanted what he wanted, but she couldn't admit it to herself—let alone him. Maybe it was time to switch tactics.

He let the silence between them lengthen again and then, shifting round, the better to watch her reaction, he said softly, 'So, are you demonstrating your independence? Or am I making you nervous?'

He had chosen his words intentionally, guessing that she would find it impossible not to rise to the implication that somehow he had got under her skin. His as-

sumption was quickly and gratifyingly confirmed as
she turned and glared at him, her narrowed gaze two
slits of hostile blue.

'Nervous! Why would I be *nervous*?'

He shrugged, watching the slow rise of colour in
her cheeks and the darkening of her eyes.

'Being here with me...' he murmured. 'Alone...
There was a time when we couldn't keep our hands
off of one another—'

He could hear her breathing, short and sharp and
shallow, and felt a shivering rush of triumph dart over
his skin. She was more than nervous. She was aroused.

'That was a long time ago,' she said stiffly. 'A lot's
changed.'

'And a lot hasn't...' He paused, feeling his body respond to the provocation in her eyes and the pulse jerking erratically at the base of her throat. 'Like this...'
And, reaching out, he stretched his arm along the back
of the seat and lightly touched her hair. 'This hasn't
changed one bit. It's still just as wild and beautiful.'
Pulling loose a gleaming curl, he wound the hair round
his finger.

Heart pounding, Addie shook his hand off. 'Actually, I've been thinking about going blonde. And short.
Really short.'

With considerable difficulty, she tore her eyes away
from his dark, shimmering gaze. Did he seriously think
that one touch was all it would take? That just stroking
her hair would be enough for her to melt into his arms
and forget all about his appalling attempt to blackmail
her? She caught her breath. Probably. He was so used

to women throwing themselves at him. And, judging by the way her whole body was vibrating like a tuning fork, it appeared that she agreed with him. Or at least her stupid, treacherous body did.

'I could walk from here,' she said quickly, glancing out of the window at the rain-spattered pavement. 'It doesn't look that bad any more.'

She turned to face him and instantly wished she hadn't. Lounging negligently, his grey gaze seemed to hold her captive, so that even if she'd wanted to yank open the door and run as fast as possible from the dangerous, swirling undercurrents in the car, she would not have been able to do so.

'What?' she said hoarsely. 'Why are you looking at me like that?'

'Why do you think?' Slowly, with almost cat-like laziness, he leaned forward and picked up her hand, playing gently with her fingers.

She opened her mouth to tell him she didn't know or care, but somehow the words stayed stubbornly in her throat. Her mouth was dry and she could feel her pulse hammering in her wrists so hard that her hands seemed like living creatures. Drawing back, she pressed her spine into the upholstery of the seat.

'It doesn't matter what I think. None of this is real.' She shook her head. 'It's like you said. It's just us being alone together again.'

He was holding her softly, but his voice was softer still. 'Maybe. Only you seem pretty damn real to me—and so does how I'm feeling right now.'

Her blood felt as though it were thinning, growing

lighter. If only she could fly, she thought desperately, fly far away. But neither fight nor flight was possible. Even thinking appeared to be a struggle.

Threads of heat were trickling slowly over her skin like warm syrup off a spoon and she stared at him helplessly, hypnotised by the languorous glow of his gaze. She wanted to lie back and close her eyes and breathe in his warm, masculine scent and believe what he was saying was true. How could it not be? When he said it in that voice…

For a moment she lingered over his words, repeating them inside her head: *How I'm feeling right now…*

And slowly she pulled her fingers away from his. It sounded true because it *was* true. Probably Malachi *did* feel like that 'right now'. But it would pass. No matter how beautiful and enticing it sounded, it was as transient as a winter sunset.

She shrank back inside her skin. 'But that doesn't make it right,' she said quietly.

She felt his gaze, fierce and fixed, on the side of her face.

'It makes it better than right. It makes it perfect. This time, this way, it'll be good between us. There's no expectation. No promises or pressure.'

He made it sound so simple, so perfect. She could feel herself wavering.

Beside her, he inched closer, and looking up into the focus of his eyes, she saw a heat and intensity that seemed to melt her breath. She felt a rush of panic for those eyes told her what she already knew: that he still owned her sexually and now he was claiming her back.

'Stop it!' She lifted her hand and held it up. 'Stop saying these things. And don't come any nearer. I don't want you to.'

'Only because you don't trust yourself.'

Holding up his hand, he pressed his palm against hers, and the longing inside her seemed to split her apart.

'Why are you fighting this? You want me as much as I want you, Addie. Tell me you don't. Tell me I'm wrong.' In the depths of his eyes something flickered like the flare of a match—a small, bright flame of desire.

She knew she should speak, deny his claim. But she couldn't find her voice—and even if she could have done she wouldn't have been able to string her words together in any sensible order.

Heat was spilling over her skin like milk boiling over in a pan. And suddenly she wanted it to overwhelm her. To stop fighting and sink beneath the liquid warmth. His fingers were wrapping around hers, tugging her inexorably towards him, and she knew that they were going to kiss and she was glad…because sometimes kisses were less complicated than words.

Reaching up, she pressed her fingers against his lips, shivering as she saw his gaze darken with hunger. For a moment their eyes locked, and then she slid her hand up and over his jaw and into his dark silky hair, pulling his mouth feverishly onto hers.

At the touch of his lips she felt an ache—blissful, voluptuous—spreading out low from her pelvis, and then her hands splayed apart, her head spinning dizzily as he deepened the kiss.

Moaning, she arched her body towards him, her breath stuttering in her throat, a fissure opening up inside her as his tongue slid between her parted lips and his hands curved around her waist and thigh, pressing, probing.

'Addie...'

She heard him murmur her name, felt his hand slide inexorably up over the soft skin of her thigh and then higher, beneath the hem of her dress to the pulse beating insistently between her legs.

Her skin felt hot and tight; inside she could feel herself melting. Gasping, she leaned against the hard muscles of his chest, the hot, salt scent of him coiling round her skin so that she was shaking with longing, her whole body clamouring for more. Shuddering, she pulled at his shirt, tugging at it where it was caught beneath his waistband, lost in the quickening of her breath and the lambent heat pooling low in her pelvis.

He groaned softly. 'Stop, sweetheart...'

And then he said it more loudly, dragging his mouth from hers, lifting his hands away, and she stared up at him dazedly even as her disorientated brain began to absorb the full facts of the situation.

Her eyes opened and, face flaming, she stared in horror at her reflection in the window. How could she have let that happen? Was she out of her mind?

But blaming her mind for what had just happened was about as senseless as blaming the moon for turning the tide. However, any debate on the whys and where-fores of blame was going to have to wait.

Taking a quick breath, she looked up at him reluctantly. 'That shouldn't have happened,' she said slowly.

Leaning back against the seat, he watched her smooth down the hem of dress. 'And yet it did.'

Her cheeks grew hotter. 'It was a mistake.'

'And we learn from our mistakes?' he said idly, reaching out to take her hand.

'I have,' she retorted. 'I've learned that I shouldn't accept lifts from strangers.'

She tried to twist her hand away from his but he tightened his grip, pulling her towards him so that her body was pressed against his.

'But I'm not a stranger. I'm your husband.'

And, lowering his head, he kissed her again. She felt the same pull as before, the same ache, only stronger, more fervent, and she moaned softly.

'Come away with me, Addie.' His eyes were dark and fierce and compelling. 'There's things we need to talk about alone. Just the two of us. Please—say yes.'

She pressed her hand against her swimming head, staring at him helplessly, hazy with wanting him, with needing him, and then finally she nodded, for the sexual attraction between them was irrefutable, so why keep trying to suppress it?

'Say it!' His hands captured her face. 'I want to hear you say it.'

She hesitated. If she half closed her eyes and her mind to the tiny, nagging voices in her head, she could almost absolve herself from any responsibility for her actions.

Her breath tangled in her throat. But if she spoke, if she went into this now, agreed to this deal, then she would do so *knowing* that Malachi didn't love her.

She shifted in her seat. Maybe it would be easier that way. There would be no more broken hearts and shattered dreams. In fact dreams would come true for the children who learned to trust and hope and believe again through music. The charity she had founded, which had brought passion and pride back to her life, would grow and prosper. And maybe she needed to own this decision unlike last time when she'd been dazzled and docile and always one step behind.

Determinedly, she lifted her chin. 'Yes. I'll come away with you.' Her employee Carmen was always begging her to take a break. She would be happy to cover for her.

She felt the car slow as he kissed her again, his hands stroking her hair. Then, breaking the kiss, he looked down at her, his face catching the light so that her breath caught in her throat at the absurdity of his perfect cheekbones.

'It's not too late to change your mind.' Despite the teasing smile, his eyes were serious.

Her heart gave a lurch and she almost laughed out loud. Of course it was too late. It had been too late ever since that letter had turned up in her in tray.

Shaking her head, she lifted her chin. 'No. You're right—we do need to talk. Besides, I could do with a holiday.'

His eyes gleamed. 'You might need another one after we get back. This one could be quite...*strenuous*.'

Before she could reply he leaned forward and tapped on the window. And she felt the car stop.

Stepping onto the pavement, Addie looked up at the sky. The rain had stopped and a small, pale sun was edging out from behind the clouds.

She turned to face him, feeling suddenly awkward. 'So what happens now?'

Reaching out, he pulled her against him, sliding his arms around her waist, and the touch of his strong hands made her heart slam against her ribs.

'You go inside and pack,' he said mockingly. 'We leave on Monday.'

'Monday!' She stared at him in shock, her ears buzzing.

He nodded. 'My driver will pick you up at nine. Try not to keep him waiting too long.'

Addie was starting to feel somewhat overwhelmed, both by the speed of these arrangements and this unsettling reminder of Malachi's wealth.

But, determined not to show her discomfort or lack of sophistication, she merely nodded. 'Leave for where? New York? France? The moon?'

Even to her own ears her voice sounded high and petulant, and she blushed as he laughed softly.

'The Caribbean. I own an island there—off Antigua.' Glancing at her astonished expression, he grinned.

'Y-you *own* an island?' She had given up trying to play it cool. 'What kind of island?'

'The usual kind.' He gave her a slow, teasing smile. 'White sand. Palm trees. Paradise on earth.'

Her head was spinning; questions were flying in every direction. But he was already back in the car.

'Wait!' Stepping forward, she hammered on the window, her breath churning in her throat as it slid down.

He leaned forward, a teasing smile on his handsome face. 'What's the matter? Are you missing me already?'

She frowned. Away from his touch, with the cooling breeze on her skin, her head was clearing. 'I need to know what to pack.'

He laughed, his eyes gleaming. 'It's a honeymoon, sweetheart. You don't need to pack anything at all!'

CHAPTER FOUR

IN THE TINY bedroom of her apartment, Addie stood staring despairingly at the half-empty holdall on her bed. She had woken early and, after nearly an hour of lying in the darkness, had finally got out of bed with the intention of being calm and collected by the time Malachi's car arrived to pick her up. Yet somehow she wasn't anywhere near ready and, pushing down the swell of panic rising inside her, she sat down on her bed with a thump.

It was all happening so fast—too fast. Three days ago she hadn't seen or spoken to Malachi for five years. Now she was going away with him for a month. Alone. Today. This morning.

The thought was like a jolt of electricity passing through her body, and mechanically she began to fold her clothes and pack them in the bag.

After Malachi had driven off she'd felt exhausted— almost as though she'd just completed some arduous Herculean challenge. Lifting her hand, she pressed her fingers to her lips, remembering the bruising heat of his kisses.

Frankly, Hercules had it easy! She'd take defeating monsters any day over trying to resist the charms of her husband who, in his own devastating way, could cause the same mayhem and misery as any three-headed dog. Unlike the three-headed dog, however, he didn't serve some angry god. He was entirely self-serving and always, however reasonable he appeared, got exactly what he wanted.

Although, to be fair, she had wanted it too. Her cheeks grew warm. More than wanted it. It had been frantic, unstoppable, an almost primeval surge of need to feel his hands on her body again, his mouth on her mouth...

And he'd been the one to pull away, and it was only later that she'd realised how close she'd come to letting him make love to her in the back of his car.

It had been a shock to discover just how much she still wanted him. But a bigger shock was the realisation that instead of shame or regret she'd felt almost elated by what had happened. Elated and aroused. She bit her lip. Since splitting up with Malachi her job had more or less taken over her life. Sometimes she went to the gym, or met friends after work. But mostly she just ate her dinner on the sofa before falling into bed alone. There certainly hadn't been any romance.

Only now she was going to spend a month on a private Caribbean island. With Malachi. A man whose touch had tormented and tamed her.

She breathed out slowly.

She was almost certainly going to regret this trip. But those few snatched moments of release in the limousine had at least proved to her what she'd known but denied for so long. That she wasn't completely over Malachi; that in some intangible, incomprehensible way she still felt married to him.

She winced. Put like that, it sounded mad. But she wasn't living under any delusions. This 'honeymoon' wasn't some last-ditch attempt to save their relationship. Quite the reverse, in fact. It was a *coda*: a bittersweet and fitting finale to a marriage that had never been quite what it seemed—to her, at least. At least this time their relationship might actually be more straightforward, more honest, despite, or maybe because it involved a simple trade-off: sex for money.

This time her heart was definitely off limits. This deal would only involve her body—and only for a limited period. And, of course, a large amount of money.

She zipped the bag shut.

Did that make her shallow? Mercenary. Immoral.

No, it did not, she thought defiantly.

She'd never asked him for anything. Not a single cent. And she still hadn't. This was for her charity. But seeing him again had made her realise that she couldn't keep avoiding the past. Finally she was ready to bring an end to all the years spent wondering, hoping, aching. And that meant being with her husband one last time. She let out a long, slow breath. So why not make the most of it?

After all, there were a lot worse ways to spend a month than being on a private island with a sexy, handsome billionaire.

At the thought of Malachi's island she felt a flicker

of fear. How was she going to survive the two of them being alone on a deserted island?

By sticking to the rules. Kissing was almost unavoidable and, knowing Malachi, if he thought she was trying to avoid kissing him he'd simply see it as a challenge. But there would be no touchy-feely stuff—the sort of things couple did without thinking—because this was a business arrangement and there was no point in blurring the boundaries.

She also expected to be treated with respect. Okay, he had the money, but this arrangement was only going to work if she made it clear that while her body might have a price she, Addie, was beyond even *his* wealth. The remnants of her pride required that she demand that at least.

And if it all got too unbearable she could always catch a plane back to Miami. She wasn't so destitute that she couldn't afford an airfare home!

Beside her on the bed her phone vibrated and, picking it up, she glanced at the screen and felt her heart jolt. The car would be arriving in twenty minutes. Just enough time to dry her hair and find her passport and double-check that Carmen knew she was in charge of the office for the next four weeks.

Thirty minutes later, wearing a short navy wraparound skirt and an embroidered cream silk blouse, she was sitting in the back of the limousine, trying her hardest to look as though it was something she did every day of her life. Tucking her legs to one side, she glanced down at her high-heeled navy court shoes and frowned. She hardly ever wore heels outside of work, and they were not the most practical footwear for a beach holiday, but she wanted a reminder of why she was there: a private nudge to herself that this was not personal but business. And, anyway, she needed the extra height if she was going to square up to Malachi's six-foot-two frame.

Feeling the car slow, she glanced out of the window and saw that they'd arrived at a large private airfield. And then her breath seemed to lodge in her throat as she saw the sleek white plane, emblazoned with the King Industries logo, gleaming on the runway. Beside it a line of stewards stood, waiting on the tarmac, all looking as though they'd just stepped out of the pages of Italian *Vogue*, and suddenly she felt like a rather unprepared understudy about to step on to a West End stage.

Who were they expecting? What had Malachi told them?

She would soon find out.

As the limousine swung smoothly to a stop and the door beside her opened she took a deep breath, swung her legs out of the car and stepped onto the tarmac.

Immediately the nearest steward walked swiftly towards her, smiling. 'Good morning, Ms Farrell. My name is John. I'm the chief steward on this flight and I will be taking care of you today. Welcome to King Airlines.'

Inside the plane, Addie had to clench her jaw to stop it from falling open. She'd flown before. She'd even been upgraded to business class once. But this—

Trying not to gawp, she gazed slowly around.

It was not like the interior of any plane she'd ever travelled on. Rather than banks of seats with a central aisle, there was a large open-plan lounge area that spanned the width of the plane. Between huge leather sofas, vases filled with freesias stood on top of mirror-topped tables. There was also a bar!

Five minutes later she was sitting at one end of a sofa, sipping a perfect cappuccino from a fine bone china cup, when a door at the end of the cabin opened and Malachi sauntered towards her across the carpet.

'Sorry, sweetheart. This trip of ours has thrown quite a few balls up into the air. I needed to meet with some people just to make sure somebody catches them while I'm away.'

Before she had a chance to reply, he dropped down onto the sofa beside her and in one seamless movement took the cup from her unprotesting hands, jerked her onto his lap and kissed her so deeply that she came up gasping for breath. He tasted of sunlight and oranges, and despite the chill of the air conditioning his skin was warm.

'I missed you.'

His eyes were fixed on her lips and his face was so golden and perfect that for a moment she couldn't even remember how to speak, let alone what to say. She looked up at him warily as he grinned down at her, the brightness of the day lighting up the shards of silver in his eyes.

'This is where you're supposed to say, *I missed you too!*' he said softly.

She felt her insides tighten, every inch of her body

responding to the pressure of his arm curling around her waist and the teasing note in his voice.

'It's only been two days.' She arched an eyebrow, hoping that she appeared more composed than she felt. 'You survived five years before that.'

'How do you know I survived?'

Something flickered across his face, too fast for her to catch.

'Maybe I was confined to bed. Weakened and distraught.'

'Then somebody very like you was out and about in Miami,' she retorted tartly. 'Attending civic functions and charity dinners. You might want to look into that when you get back. Identity theft is a serious business!'

His eyes glittered. 'I'm flattered you kept such a close eye on my whereabouts—'

'I did not—' she protested, but her voice frayed, the hot seam of words unravelling as his hand brushed against her blouse.

'I like this,' he murmured, fingering the silk. 'It's kind of demure yet sexy.'

As his gaze drifted slowly over her legs and down to her shoes, his eyes hardened in a way that made her stomach start to spasm.

'And I like those too.'

His hand slipped beneath her blouse, cool fingers sliding over her hot skin so that she stirred against him, feeling the shift in his breathing. And then, abruptly, he groaned and, gently tipping her off his lap and back onto the sofa, edged away from her.

'Damn it, Addie!' He was grimacing as though in pain.

'What is it?' She stared up at him dizzily, her head still reeling from the havoc his fingers had wrought upon her, feeling the absence of his warm body almost like an amputation.

Shaking his head, he gave her a wry smile. 'I've got a room full of people back there, waiting for me to sign off on a business plan, and you've got me so het up I'm not sure I can even spell my name—let alone write it.'

It took a couple of seconds for her to register what he was saying. That she would have to wait. Meeting his gaze, she saw the soft, taunting glimmer in his grey eyes and felt her temper start to flare. Was that how it was going to be? Him taking every opportunity to remind her that he was the one calling the shots.

Of course it was.

Right from the start Malachi had been the one dictating the terms of their arrangement. And, typical Malachi, he'd done it with a slow, teasing smile on that handsome face of his. And so of course, now she was here on his private jet, the ultimate symbol of his wealth and power, he would make her wait—presumably to demonstrate that no matter how equal the sexual attraction between them was, *he* was always in charge.

It was all she could do to stay sitting on the sofa. But she couldn't keep threatening to walk out on him like some Hollywood diva who didn't like her dressing room. The fact was she had agreed to this ludicrous charade, and she'd known right from the start that he was going to enjoy tormenting her. Her skin tightened as she remembered exactly how good he was at tormenting her. How he'd used to love to keep her hanging on so that she was frantic, wild, almost out of her mind with sexual need.

Dragging her mind back to the present, she gritted her teeth. The mature response—the *only* response— was not to dignify it with any response at all and so not give him the satisfaction of knowing that he'd got under her skin. But just because she'd agreed to come on this trip, it didn't mean she was some sort of concubine. She just needed to find a way to remind Malachi of that fact.

For a moment they stared at one another in silence, and then finally she shrugged. 'It's fine. I can entertain myself,' she said, reaching into her handbag. She pulled out a large paperback book. 'I thought this might come in useful on this trip,' she said sweetly.

His eyes locked on to hers.

'*Emotional Intelligence in the Adolescent Mind.* Sounds gripping. But I thought you were here to mess with my body. Not my mind.'

The thought of what form that *messing* might take made Addie's tongue stick to the roof of her mouth, but despite her hot cheeks she lifted her chin to stare at him. 'It's actually very interesting and informative,' she said loftily.

'I'm sure it is.' His eyes mocked her and, blowing her a kiss, he turned and sauntered out of the cabin.

He was back in less than half an hour. As he strode across the carpet every inch of him was humming with energy, like a racing car on the starting grid.

'All done!' His voice was hard with triumph. Collapsing onto the cushions beside her, he leaned over and picked up a handful of strawberries, tearing into them with white, even teeth. 'And now you have my full and undivided attention.' He plucked the book from her hand and dropped it casually onto the nearest table. 'Now, where were we?' His gaze slid down over her face, down lower to the pulse beating at the base of her throat. 'Oh, yes… Why don't you come over here and sit back on my lap?'

She stared at him in silence, too angry to reply in case she lost her temper. Did he think he could just swan back in and click his fingers and she'd come running? That she'd drop whatever she was doing or have it dropped by him.

She glanced across at the book. *Take control!* she told herself. *Show him that he can't walk all over you. He might have the plane and the limo and the money—especially the money. But he can't have you, not unless he works for it!*

'I've got a better idea,' she said slowly. Standing up, she smoothed her skirt over her thighs, watching his eyes drift down to the hem and then back up to meet her face.

'Why don't we get out of here? Go somewhere a little more private?' His gaze was suddenly so focused, so intense, it made her stomach curl into a knot. But, ignoring the pulse leaping in her throat, she smiled at him coolly. 'Shall I just pick a door? Or do you want to show me the way?'

Staring straight ahead, she kept her eyes glued to his broad back as Malachi led her up a floating spiral staircase to what must be the private quarters of the plane. She held her breath. He wasn't even touching her but already her skin was quivering, the blood slowing and thickening in her veins. She wanted him so badly—but more than that she wanted him to want her as much, even more than she craved him. To be in thrall to her. She wanted to have power over him, to get past that mask and beneath that beautiful, lazy smile and see that formidable self-control slip away.

Her muscles gave an involuntary twitch. They had reached the top of the staircase. There was a moment of tense, pulsing silence and then, pushing open a door, he stepped aside. After a fraction of a second she walked past him. It was another, slightly smaller lounge. There were a couple of gilt-framed mirrors on the walls and on top of several narrow, pale wood tables piles of paperback books vied with one another for space. Looking up, she found Malachi watching her, his eyes more black now than grey, and she felt her body respond to their darkening.

'So,' he said softly. 'Here we are. "Somewhere more private".'

His words snagged on her skin and, pulse jerking, she nodded, trying to stay calm. 'It feels different. Less—'

'Flashy?' For a moment he looked younger, more earnest.

'I was going to say formal,' she said carefully.

He laughed. 'How worryingly diplomatic of you.' He stared past her. 'Downstairs is just an extension of my office. It has to present a certain version of me. Up here is mine.'

Some of his tension had slipped away and she stared around, liking the comfort and the easy elegance. 'What's through there?' She gestured to a door at the other end of the room.

'It's a gym and a steam room.'

'What about up there?' She pointed to more curving steps that seemed to hang magically in the air. There was a moment of pulsing silence. He turned and his gaze slipped over her skin like warm silk. Suddenly she could feel her blood racing through her body like wild mustangs.

'Come and see.' He held out his hand.

She stared at it for a moment, letting his words hang in the air, needing a moment to clear her head of the pulsing beat of her heart.

Do it, she urged herself again. *Do it on your terms. Take control.*

Taking his hand, she slipped past him, turning at the bottom of the staircase. 'I think I can find my way from here.'

She walked up the stairs slowly, his hand clasped in hers. At the top she stopped and stared—at a bed.

But only for a moment.

Then she turned and reached for him, her fingers curling into the fabric of his shirt, grabbing, tugging, pulling at buttons and hair and flesh. She'd caught him off guard, could feel he shook. But the next moment his mouth was on hers, fierce, bruising, heavy. Desperately she kissed him back, locking her arms around his neck, frantic with the freedom of being able to touch him, to kiss him, to run her fingers through his hair.

Catching the scent of his skin, she moaned softly, and her breath quickened as she felt his body move urgently against hers. She heard him groan and felt a rush of euphoria, and then suddenly his hands were on her waist, pushing her back and across the floor, his legs nudging and pressing between hers. She half slid, half fell onto the bed, pulling him with her, her mouth opening beneath the hard pressure of his lips.

His hands were at her waist, her thighs, her ribs— sliding all over her body, peeling away her shirt and her defences. Her breath felt hot in her throat, the tormenting touch of his mouth making her head swim and, moaning, she reached lower, pressing her hand against the smooth muscles of his stomach until she felt his body shudder.

'Malachi!' She whispered his name unsteadily and breathing in hard, she stilled as he raised himself up and stared down into her face, his grey eyes gleaming like polished steel.

'What's the matter?' he murmured. 'Have you lost your way?'

Addie shuddered. His fingertips, light and languid, were sliding over the smooth mound of her belly, stroking, circling, caressing lower, and lower still, so that a tingling, torturous thread of pleasure wove in and out of her breathing.

Suddenly he lifted his hand and she couldn't stop herself from whimpering. His gaze fixed on her face, his expression so hard and hungry and knowing that she squirmed against the sheets. There was no way to hide how much she wanted him to keep on touching her, how much she needed to feel him on top and inside her.

'Malachi…' She swallowed, fighting to control the need, the urgency in her voice, trying to hang on to the liquid heat building inside her, her muscles clenching and tightening.

'Addie—'

He let the word hang between them as she looked up at him pleadingly and then, lowering his head, he licked her shoulder, his tongue hot and measured as it snaked over her collarbone, teasing the hollow at the base of her throat until her body started to shake.

His fingers spread across the bare skin of her back, expertly undoing her bra and freeing her swollen, aching breasts. Almost choking on her own breath, she twisted upwards, rubbing against his hips, goading him with her body, wanting him to answer the ache clamouring inside her. But, pushing aside the flimsy fabric, he dropped his head and grazed her breast with his mouth, licking and nipping, his tongue curling around first one nipple then the other.

Finally she could bear it no more and she pushed his head away, at the same time desperately reaching beneath the waistband of his trousers to curl her hand round the hard, straining length of his erection.

He jerked against her, his breath coming in ragged gasps. Grasping her head, he began to kiss her again, each time deeper and deeper, until she thought she would melt with need. A slippery heat was trickling down inside her and helplessly she rolled beneath him, wanting to rid herself of that relentless, dragging ache, wanting, needing to feel him inside, *to finish what she'd started.*

She tugged at his belt urgently, her fingers tearing at the buckle, scraping his skin.

'Wait—wait, sweetheart. We mustn't—'

His hand caught her scrabbling fingers, holding them still, and she stared up at him dazedly.

'Wh-what?' Fighting to get her words out, she frowned. A haze of unfocused thoughts and fears were swirling inside her head. 'What do you mean?' Her voice was hoarse. She could hear her hunger for him, the scraped, raw longing. But she didn't care. She just wanted him—all of him. The heat and the power, the unthinkable, impossible bliss of his body stretching into hers.

He shook his head. 'Not here. Not now.'

She looked up at him, shifting restlessly, her whole body twitching with unfulfilled desire so that she had to bite her tongue in order not to beg him to make love to her.

His hand was curving under the back of her head so that his calm, assessing grey gaze held her captive. For a moment he studied her face and then, raising his hips, he let go of her hand and lifting himself off her body, he slid onto the bed beside her.

The cool air stung her skin.

But not as much as the cool, calculating expression on Malachi's face.

How could he look at her like that? She stared at him uneasily. And how had he found the willpower to stop? The thought that, unlike her, he had been cool-headed enough to break their frantic, febrile embrace was like a punch to the stomach. Cheeks burning, she breathed in sharply and pushed against his shoulder.

He made no objection as she shifted along the bed, tugging at her bra and blouse and pushing her skirt down over her naked thighs, shock at her own behaviour mingling with the humiliating realisation that, rather than taking charge, she had let her self-control go into a complete and very obvious meltdown. It had not been *him* begging *her* to ease the frantic demands of *his* body. Instead she had been the one whose whole being had been focused on satisfying her burning desire for him.

A discreet but insistent buzzing noise broke the silence between them and, rolling over, Malachi punched a button on a panel set into the wall above the bed.

'Yes.'

'Sorry, Mr King. Just to let you know we are approaching Antigua now, so if you wouldn't mind buckling up?'

'Yes, of course.' Hanging up, Malachi turned and met her gaze. 'We'd better go and take our seats.'

Smoothing his fingers through his hair, he tucked in his shirt and as though by magic was transformed back into a sleek, efficient business tycoon.

His eyes drifted over her dishevelled state. 'You might want to tidy up a little...'

Staring at her reflection in the bathroom mirror, Addie mechanically ran a comb through her hair. Her hand was shaking too much to put on any lipstick or eye make-up, so instead she tried to force her face into the same cool mask of detachment that Malachi could apparently achieve so effortlessly.

How did he do it? she thought helplessly. Even now, with her clothes straightened and buttoned up, and a door between them, her body was still a shuddering mass of sexual yearning, her brain barely functioning.

She moaned softly. She had so wanted to prove to him, to herself, that no matter how disparate their wealth and status they would come together as sexual equals on this trip. But the harsh reality was that she had simply managed to reveal how badly she still wanted him. She'd responded to him mindlessly, her hunger so intense, so desperate that she'd been ready and willing to surrender herself to his every whim—

She shivered. The trouble was that she couldn't do what he did. She couldn't blank off her mind from the passion, the hunger. How could she? Until her car accident her whole life had been about living emotions through music. Playing the piano demanded passion as much as discipline, poetry as much as practice.

Her mouth twisted. Sex with Malachi was evidently not going to be as straightforward as she'd thought. Not because she loved him. But because she appeared unable to switch off the mess of emotion that sex with Malachi provoked.

Her heart began to pound. But so what if she couldn't contain or control her feelings? Did she really want to become like Malachi? All warmth and charm on the outside, but utterly immune to real feelings.

No, she did not.

Her marriage to Malachi had already cost her five

years of her life, her hopes, most of her pride and around six kilograms of weight. She wasn't about to sacrifice the essence of who she was to it too.

And she *would* survive this trip.

After all, she'd survived far worse.

Lifting her chin, she pulled out a lipstick and swiped it over her lips. She might come out of this affair emotionally battered and bruised, but she would come out of it as herself.

Turning, she pushed open the bathroom door and walked determinedly back into the cabin.

'Ready?' His voice was distracted, his eyes fixed on the screen of his phone.

She cleared her throat and waited for him to look up, watching his eyes narrow appreciatively as they switched from his phone to her glossy lips and long bare legs.

She met his gaze. 'I've never been readier,' she said slowly.

CHAPTER FIVE

STARING OUT ACROSS the turquoise-blue sea, Malachi felt a ripple of satisfaction break over his skin. Beside him in the speedboat Addie sat gazing out across the water, her long red hair blowing across her face, her slender legs curling against the smooth suede upholstery. He could imagine how they must appear to everyone around them: the perfect honeymooning couple on their way to paradise.

Beneath his expensive sunglasses his eyes glittered. Except that they weren't. Yes, his wife was *there*, her warm, seductive body just inches away from his. But, glancing at the pure line of her profile, he knew that her thoughts were far away. No doubt dealing with the unfamiliar sting of having her warm, seductive body turned down.

He shifted in his seat, his groin tightening uncomfortably. It might be rather more painful than he'd anticipated but he'd proved his point. She wanted him—and badly. Remembering those blue eyes dilating in helpless response, her body twitching beneath his, he felt a rush of triumph. Only it was tempered with a slight sense of relief, for he had come dangerously close to taking her there and then and he hated feeling that frantic. It was too raw a reminder of how his life had used to be, watching and waiting for his parents' parties finally to end.

But soon he would ease his body into hers. Only for now let *her* be the one feeling out of control.

As though sensing his thoughts, she glanced up and gave him an icy glare.

'Everything all right?' he said softly.

He watched her fingers curl into her hands.

'Everything's fine.'

'Really? Only you seem a little tense.' He gazed at her levelly. 'Is it the boat? I could rub your back if you think it would help…'

Oh, she was tense, all right. She'd tried and failed to cover it up, for he'd noticed the wary uncertainty in her eyes, the nervous flush of colour in her cheeks the moment she'd walked out of the bathroom. But there was no place on this trip for feelings—*her* feelings, for of course his weren't ever going to be a problem. He'd learned the hard way that life and particularly relationships were simpler, smoother, sweeter all round if emotions were removed from the equation.

His eyes fixed dispassionately on a distant speck of green and brown, rising out of the sea, and his mouth curled into a tight smile. It was the face he presented to any unfortunate gambler who got caught breaking the rules at his casinos.

And Addie had broken the rules. The first rule of the house.

She'd interfered with the run of play.

His mouth thinned. Or rather he'd *let* her interfere with it. Let her catch him off guard.

Beside her, Addie felt Malachi move, but she ignored him. She was still fuming over that last remark. Rub her back? She'd rather jump overboard. Or better still push him in. For a moment she allowed herself to picture Malachi walking a plank.

Imagining the splash he would make greatly restored her spirits and, feeling able to face him again, she looked up and said sweetly, 'Everything all right with you?'

'Everything is fine.'

'Really? Only you seem a little restless,' she said.

He held her gaze. 'I was just thinking about poker.'

She glowered at him. Typical! So nothing had changed. She was still three steps behind him and he was thinking about cards. Carefully she turned her body away from his.

Gazing past Addie, remembering again how close he'd come to losing control, Malachi frowned. He'd been completely unprepared for the way she'd taken his hand and led him upstairs. More mind-blowing still had been how she'd kissed him. The touch of her lips on his had been like napalm—a flash of raw white heat, explosive, all-consuming. He'd been out of control, reduced to no more than a pulsing mass of heat and longing. And for that moment he'd wanted whatever she wanted and more.

His stomach clenched. Before he'd met Addie his mantra for living had been simple: work hard, play harder. By sheer effort and determination he'd transformed his family's casino business from a debt-ridden mess into a global brand. And to relax there had been women. All beautiful, sexy and disposable.

Until five years ago. Until Addie.

When, despite knowing exactly how damaging and abusive marriage could be, he'd gone ahead and married her. And he still couldn't quite understand why. It didn't make sense, not after his childhood with its ringside seat at his parents' marriage. Watching helplessly as they'd let sex and passion twist their lives—*and his.* He'd sworn never to do the same. A muscle tightened in his jaw.

But Addie had been so beautiful, so tempting, with that glorious red hair tangling about shoulders, her blue eyes pulling him in and under her spell, and just like that his promises had turned to air. Ignoring all his instincts, and every promise he'd ever made, he'd followed his libido up the aisle and married Addie, justifying it as a *commercial* decision: a merger of bodies rather than business.

It had sounded good inside his head—so good that he'd let himself believe it was the whole truth until, too late, he'd realised the scale of his mistake—and how badly sex had clouded his judgement.

But he wasn't going to let that happen again.

This time he held all the cards. He wasn't blind to the allure of her body, but this time it would be safely contained. Their arrangement would last a month, and there would be no meaningless romantic gloss. It would be like any other business arrangement. Only instead of paperwork and conference calls it would just be the two of them on a deserted island and a month of pure pleasure, designed to exorcise the sexual hold she still had over him.

Feeling suddenly immensely satisfied, he leaned towards Addie and pointed to where the dark clump of palm trees and other green foliage was rapidly growing larger.

'That's it. That's where we're going. Bar Jack Cay.'

She nodded and managed to give him a small, polite smile. But her head was spinning, her skin flushing hot then cold. It felt like seasickness but it wasn't. It was humiliation. Sitting in silence, gazing out across the water, she'd been able to pretend that she was on some other boat, maybe with friends. Those blush-making moments on the plane pushed to the back of her mind. But now that he'd spoken to her, his body leaning in, the faint smell of his cologne mingling with the sea spray, the whole embarrassing scene filled her head again.

What had she been *thinking*? She couldn't have made a bigger fool of herself if she'd planned it. Shrinking back against the seat, she felt her stomach twist with misery as she remembered her frantic behaviour, how desperate she must have looked. She might as well have worn a huge sign saying *'My sex-life is non-existent'* around her neck.

But far worse was the way she'd let him manipulate her all over again. Just as she'd done five years ago. She felt a rush of anger. Everything was such a mess, but one thing was clear. That despite what he'd said, or what they'd agreed, this arrangement clearly had more to do with power than desire. His power over her.

It was the first time she'd really understood what she had actually agreed to.

Her heart gave a jolt as the speedboat began to slow. Looking up, she found him watching her, and something in his cool, speculative gaze made her lift her eyes to meet his.

'Are we slowing down for a reason?' Her voice sounded curt, not at all like a bride on her honeymoon. But she didn't care. He was paying for her body—not for her to look as though she was madly in love with him. And it wasn't as though he would comment on her manner. He shied away from conversations that even hinted at the intimate or the personal.

With a chill, she remembered how he had refused even to acknowledge her doubts about their marriage. Like when she'd tried to find out why his parents weren't coming to the wedding. At first, he'd ignored her questions. Then finally, when she'd made it clear she wasn't going to drop the subject, he'd simply walked away. It had been the same at the reception, when having overheard a conversation about his motives for marrying, she had attempted to discuss it with him. He had withdrawn not just physically but emotionally and that was when she had known their marriage would never work.

But there was no point in thinking about any of that now and, feeling his gaze on her face, she curled her arms around her waist, flattening out the emotion inside her.

'There are rocks up ahead.' He smiled, his eyes dancing maliciously. 'You can't see them, but they'd scuttle a boat this big. So we have to transfer to a dinghy.'

Ignoring his hand, she stepped past him into the smaller boat and, laughing softly, he sat down next to her, trapping her thigh against his, his arm draping around her shoulder as she stared mutinously down at the sea.

'I know the water's tempting, sweetheart, but don't you want to look at where you're going to be staying for the next few weeks?' he teased. 'Or are you trying to work out if you can swim home?'

Gritting her teeth, Addie lifted her head reluctantly and gazed at the island.

Up close, it wasn't quite what she'd been expecting. It was beautiful in a rugged kind of way, but truthfully, she had been expecting something a little more Robinson Crusoe.

But so what if the island was a little less pretty than her mental image of paradise? It was obviously completely untouched, which was surely closer to the true meaning of paradise. Surprised that Malachi would be sensitive enough to recognise that fact, she felt some of her anger fade.

'It's beautiful,' she said stiffly, managing a small, tight smile.

Smiling back at her, he reached out, and before she could protest he had taken her hand in his. 'I like to think of it as a little bit of Eden. Somewhere I can be completely uninhibited.'

Mesmerised by the shimmering molten heat of his voice, she wondered how such a short sentence could contain so much promise of pleasure and danger.

But of course paradise wasn't perfect, she thought dully. As well as cool streams and sunshine there were snakes. Or in this case one particular snake.

But as the dinghy slid through a narrow gap in the rocks she completely forgot her doubts, for in front of her was the most beautiful beach she had ever seen. At the end of a shell-shaped pool of clear blue water was a large curve of pale gold sand, fringed with picture-book palm trees. For a moment she stared in silence, struggling to find words to put into a coherent sentence as Malachi watched her stunned reaction.

'Is it a lagoon?' she said finally.

He nodded, his face impassive but his eyes suddenly intent. 'I'm guessing this is more what you were expecting to see.'

Before she could reply he lifted his hand and waved at a man and woman who were waiting at the end of a short wooden jetty.

'That's Terry Clarke and his wife, Leonda. They take care of everything on the island. Maintenance. Laundry. Cleaning. And Leonda enjoys cooking, so anything you fancy just tell her and she'll make it. But don't worry!' His eyes mocked her. 'We'll have plenty of time on our own, sweetheart. And plenty of space. Sixteen acres, in fact. Although not all of it is accessible.'

Sliding his arm around her waist, he pulled her against him.

'Imagine it. Just you and me in paradise. Alone. Doing whatever we want.'

His eyes seemed to reach inside her and suddenly her whole body was squirming with a flickering, treacherous heat. She didn't need to imagine what she wanted to do with Malachi. Since meeting him in the restaurant it had been playing inside her head like a slow motion erotic film.

But thankfully at that moment the dinghy bumped gently against the jetty, and with relief she climbed out of the boat and away from the gravitational pull of his gaze.

Terry and his wife, Leonda, were both charming. Having grown up on Antigua, they were well informed and enthusiastic about the Caribbean island experience. Still slightly stunned by the thought that this idyllic paradise was going to be her holiday home, Addie hardly managed to do anything other than make a few polite, meaningless remarks about the colour of the sand and her fondness for mangoes. Not that it mattered. Their attention was fixed on Malachi, and who could blame them when his handsome face looked so absurdly flawless in the pure, white sunlight?

Finally they were alone.

'The villa is this way!'

Pushing aside a tangle of foliage, Malachi stepped aside to let her pass.

Addie breathed in sharply. She had thought that nothing could surpass that first view of the beach, but the villa was quite simply stunning. A clean-lined, contemporary house, set on a bleached wood deck, it was surrounded by lush grape trees and looked across another, smaller lagoon.

'There used to be a colonial-style building here, but after Hurricane Helena came we had to rebuild everything. I actually prefer the look of this. It feels less intrusive. Come on, I'll show you around.'

Inside the villa, Addie had to pinch herself. It was luxury on a scale she'd never imagined, let alone seen. Five years ago Malachi had been wealthy, but his casino empire had only just started to expand, and although the money had been there it had been in the background. Gazing round at the state-of-the-art kitchen, at the understated glamour of the lounge area and the marbled luxury of the bathroom, she started to realise just how much he had changed over the last five years.

Watching her eyes widen at the sight of the huge open-plan living area, with its linen-covered sofas and vases of frangipani, Malachi felt his stomach twist. In the way of all wealthy and sophisticated people, most of the men and women of his acquaintance would have made a concerted effort not to notice, much less remark on their surroundings. But why? What was so wrong about being open and honest?

His eyes narrowed. He must have been out too long in the sun if he had to even ask himself that question. And while it might be amusing—charming, even—to listen to Addie go into raptures over the view from his bedroom window, it reminded him why their relationship had failed. Why it could never have worked. Her fervour for life was fine when carefully managed, as part of the overall package he had envisaged for their marriage. It had even played out well with the media, giving him a new, warmer, more caring image. But that was where it should have stayed. In public. He had no use for uncontrolled emotional outbursts in his private life.

No use for it.

No understanding of it.

And definitely no need for it.

'What's that over there?'

Addie's voice broke into his thoughts and, turning, he looked towards where she was pointing, over the lagoon to a wavering white line cut through the verdant foliage.

'I think it's a waterfall.' He squinted across the water. 'I seem to remember there being one.'

She frowned at him. 'How can you not know if there's a waterfall?'

He frowned. 'I *do* know. I just can't remember if that's where it is. I haven't been round the island for years. When I stay I don't generally bother leaving the villa. I don't need to. There's enough to keep me entertained here.'

She gritted her teeth. By 'enough', he clearly meant some eager, sexually responsive female companion. It was a surprisingly unwelcome discovery, although she hadn't for one moment imagined that he had been single for the last five years. But did he have to rub in that fact here, now?

'If you're expecting some kind of sexual Olympics then I think you might be in for a disappointment,' she said tartly. 'Maybe you should have brought whichever woman you normally come here with instead.'

He stared at her in silence and then, smiling slowly, he leaned forward. 'You're the first and only woman I've ever brought here, sweetheart. The first and only I've ever *wanted* to bring here.'

It was true. He usually only visited the island on his way to or from a business trip, and he had certainly never brought a woman. Not even his mother. *Especially not my mother*, he thought grimly.

'I come here four or five times a year. As a reward for sitting through interminable discussions with people I'm only meeting so they remember my face.'

He smiled at her slowly, and suddenly her mouth was dry and her heart was pounding against her ribs. People didn't forget a man like Malachi King, his dark, restless gaze and pure, clean profile. And they always remembered his slow, devastating smile. She knew just how far someone would go to make Malachi King smile like that—and how much they would be prepared to sacrifice.

She had the scars to prove it.

The watch on his wrist made two small beeping noises and, grateful for the chance to break free of the tension swelling between them, she took hold of his arm and turned it gently.

'Is that the time?' she said quickly. 'No wonder I feel so hungry. Why don't we go down and I'll see if I can rustle up something to eat?'

Frowning, he pressed his hand against his forehead.

'I completely forgot. Leonda told me she'd left us some lunch. Nothing fancy, but I'm sure it'll be delicious.'

It was. A three-course cold buffet, all exquisitely presented. Leonda had also thoughtfully provided a handwritten menu, listing all the ingredients.

'I can't believe I offered to cook,' Addie groaned, gazing down at her plate.

'You didn't.' Biting into a barbecued rib with guava and tamarind, Malachi raised an eyebrow. 'You offered to *"rustle up something".*'

He was impossible to resist. She tried to frown, but ended up smiling. 'You tricked me. You said she *enjoyed* cooking.'

His grey eyes gleamed. 'And she does. She also happens to be a Cordon Bleu trained cook who enjoys "creating dishes which combine colonial and Caribbean influences",' he drawled. 'Or so it said on her CV.' Grinning, he leaned across and speared a small, golden parcel. 'What is *this*?'

Addie glanced at the menu. 'It's coconut and shrimp tempura. It's delicious.' She sighed. 'I think I've eaten about forty already.'

He glanced across the table. 'Only another seventy to go, then.' He grimaced. 'I'm afraid Leonda seems to think I don't eat between visits, so she always cooks enough for a small army.'

Putting her knife and fork together tidily on her plate, Addie gave him a small, careful smile. As if her feelings were as easy to arrange as her cutlery. In her head being alone with Malachi had seemed quite straightforward: there was the sex and then there was everything else. She wasn't deluded enough to pretend that she wouldn't enjoy the sex part, but she hadn't expected the talking, the just being together to be anything other than extremely trying.

Only sitting opposite him now, it was hard to feel like that. Not just because he was stupidly good-looking, but because he was such effortless company. He was bright and well read and, mixing as he did with the rich and the famous, he had an endless supply of amusing and salacious stories.

But, while she might not hate him as much as she would or perhaps should, she needed to make sure their relationship had recognisable boundaries. Sex, by necessity, involved some amount of intimacy—maybe even a certain amount of tenderness. But this—the being together part—required her to be no more than civil. In fact, now might be a good time for her to introduce a more formal, less personal tone to their lunch.

Picking up her water glass, she took a breath and said quickly, 'Thank you.'

There was a flicker of surprise in his eyes as they met hers. 'For what?'

'For bringing me here. It's lovely. Truly.' She glanced out across the lagoon. 'So how did you find this place? I mean, it's so hidden away.'

He shrugged. 'It was an accident, really. I was actually looking to buy a yacht.'

She stared at him dazedly. He spoke about buying a yacht as though it was a carton of milk. And what kind of person chose whether to buy an island or a yacht? It was just another reminder of the differences between them.

She shook her head. 'So what happened?'

His eyes gleamed. 'I went for a swim.'

She stared at him, confused. Surely he couldn't have swam that far out to sea?

Glancing at her face, Malachi shook his head. 'Not here. In a hotel. In Vegas.'

Her eyes narrowed. 'How has that got anything to do with this island?'

He gave her a teasing smile. 'I was playing poker and Teddy Chalmers—do you remember Teddy?'

Addie nodded. She had met him socially with Malachi. He was a lanky middle-aged Texan real estate billionaire, with a penchant for land and property and a passion for poker.

'Teddy bet me this island that I couldn't jump into a pool at the hotel and touch the bottom.'

She frowned. 'That's crazy. Anyone could do that.' Her face stilled with suspicion. 'So why did he think you couldn't?'

Malachi grinned. 'Probably because of the sharks!'

'Sharks!' She stared at him in horror. 'Real sharks? With teeth?'

He laughed. 'The sharks were real, so I guess their teeth were too.'

Addie gazed at him, open-mouthed.

Smiling, Malachi reached for the wine bottle and refilled his glass. 'Don't look so worried, sweetheart. I won.'

'What if you'd been bitten?'

He gave her an infuriating smile. 'I'm touched that you care.'

'I don't care,' she said quickly. 'I just can't believe you'd risk your life over some stupid bet.'

'I like to win.'

She glared at him. 'Winning isn't everything. And if you'd walked away what would you really have lost?'

He shrugged. 'My pride! Look, they were small nurse sharks in a tank in a Vegas hotel. Honestly, I didn't think it was that risky. All I really had to do was focus on winning.'

Then Teddy Chalmers must be more stupid than he appeared, Addie thought slowly. Malachi might be the most charming person she had ever met, but he was also the most driven. Losing was simply not an option for him.

He held her gaze. 'I don't make a habit of it,' he said lightly. 'But I was twenty-four years old and I'd spent the best part of a year playing poker non-stop.' He breathed out slowly. 'And with those guys everything turned into a bet.'

Picking up his wine glass, he swirled the contents slowly around.

'When I finally came out here, though, it blew me away. Not the beach and the palm trees so much. But the peace—' His mouth twisted. 'There's something so pure about the sound of the waves, and the breeze and the birdsong.'

Something in his tone made her hold her breath. She stared at him, confused. Birdsong? Since when had that mattered to Malachi? Her heart gave a thump as she wondered what else he hadn't told her. But could she blame him? She'd hardly been open or honest with him, choosing to share only a carefully edited selection of details about her accident and home life.

Staring past him, she realised that they had never really known one another at all. That they had never trusted one another enough to do so. But why be so secretive now? It wasn't as if it mattered any more.

She glanced back at his face. 'I'm not usually a big fan of peace and quiet,' she said hesitantly. 'But this is the good kind.'

'The good kind? What's the *bad* kind?' he prompted, his gaze fixed on her face, searching, curious.

She gave him a small, tight smile. It was so tempting to believe that he was genuinely interested. Had she not known him as well as she did, she might even have hoped that he felt more than just a physical attraction. That he cared about her. But she knew that for Malachi a confidence shared was just a weakness to exploit. Only given their situation, what was there left for him to exploit?

She shrugged. 'I guess when I say "bad" I mean boring.' Pausing, she frowned, her sudden impulse to be open faltering in the face of his dark, dispassionate gaze. 'Which is what I'm being now, so—'

For a moment he stared at her in silence, and then slowly he reached out and pushed a strand of hair behind her ear. 'You might be a lot of things, sweetheart. Some of them are *exceedingly* challenging.' He smiled slowly. 'But I can safely say you have never once bored me.'

Her heart twitched, caught his smile like a fish on a hook. 'It's early yet,' she said lightly.

He grinned. 'Come on, I'm intrigued.'

She burst out laughing. 'Fine. But it's really not that exciting.' She hesitated. Except that it felt stupidly exciting to be talking to him about herself. To feel his eyes on her face, not as part of some kind of foreplay but because he was listening, actually listening to her. 'I suppose it's being here. It's made me think about the holidays I used to go on with my parents.'

'Where did you go?'

'To my aunt and uncle's farm in South Dakota. Every year for years. In the mornings my mum and my aunt would sew, and my dad and uncle would fix things, and in the afternoons they would all play bridge.'

Malachi nodded. 'It's a good game. Old-timers usually play a tight hand.'

Addie smiled. 'Not just old-timers. I play a pretty tight hand too.'

'But you didn't? Play, I mean? You said, "*they* would all play bridge".'

She stiffened. No wonder he was so good at poker. He missed nothing. Every glance, every word, every blink was noted and examined and weighed up.

She shook her head. 'No. I used to help my aunt feed the animals, and then I'd do my piano practice on this old keyboard my uncle rigged up in the barn. To be honest, it wasn't really that different to being at home—just quieter. Even quieter than in Wichita.'

'I've been to Wichita.' His face was calm, watchful. 'It's not Vegas, but it's not exactly a ghost town.'

Picking up her glass, she took a sip of water, her cheeks suddenly warm. She had never told him much about her family. She hadn't wanted him to know. Beside his glamour and raw animal energy, her home, her childhood, had felt so *ordinary* and she'd been embarrassed. But mostly she'd been scared. Scared that somehow he would see through her, past whatever it was that he thought he saw, and realise her ordinariness. For deep down she had never quite believed that he wanted her for who she *really* was.

She smiled. 'Wichita is fine. It was my home that was so quiet. You see, my parents were already old when I was born. My dad was nearly sixty when my mum got pregnant. I don't remember him ever being well. I always had to be quiet at home because he was sleeping, and I couldn't have friends over to play.' She smiled again, more weakly. 'I think that's why I got so good at the piano. My lessons at my teacher's house were the only time I was allowed to be rowdy!'

'Moving to Miami must have been a bit of a shock, then.' He was smiling still, but his eyes on her face were serious.

She nodded, wondering where he was heading with that remark.

'I suppose,' she agreed. 'But in a good way. I could be who I wanted to be. The real me. And Miami is such a warm, vibrant place. It's like there's a permanent party happening.'

The change in him was negligible. She might not

even have noticed it but for the slight tightening of his mouth, the ripple of tension in his shoulders.

There was a small pause, and then he shrugged. 'You can get tired of partying!'

She looked up at his face, wishing that there were subtitles running across his forehead to give her a clue as to what was going on inside his head.

'I suppose you can,' she said carefully. 'I haven't actually been to that many.'

He shifted in his seat, abruptly switching his gaze across the veranda to the rippling blue water.

'I must have been to hundreds,' he said softly. 'My parents live to party. When I was a child, Henry, my father, kept a whole bunch of suites at the Colony Club. All weekend it would be open house. To get in, my parents just had to like you. My mother, Serena, once invited the boy who cleaned our pool because he could charm snakes.'

His face grew still and taut.

'He had other *charms* too!' He stared past her, then shrugged again. 'But not enough to keep my mother entertained. So somebody threw him out of a window. He landed in the swimming pool.' Glancing at Addie's horrified expression, he smiled tightly. 'I expect you're grateful they didn't come to our wedding now!'

She stared at him in silence. Yes and no. For a moment she considered asking him about their absence again, but the fierce dark glow in his eyes held her back.

'Wow! They don't sound like most people's parents,' she said finally.

His eyes narrowed. 'They're not. In fact I don't really think of them as parents. Serena was only sixteen when she had me, and Henry had just been kicked out of Dartmouth.' His mouth twisted. 'You could say we grew up together. And now there's a couple of calls I need to make, so why don't you take a shower or go for a swim?'

Disconcerted, she met his gaze. But there was no mistaking the discouraging tone of his voice. Nor the shuttered look in his eyes. The conversation was over.

In the end she took the shower. An hour later she lay on the bed, gazing out of the window. It had certainly been an interesting day. So much had happened—what with all the travelling and her failed attempt to seduce Malachi on the plane. Only even that felt so long ago now, and suddenly far less significant, pushed aside by his unexpected and uncharacteristic revelations about his life.

Thinking back to what he'd told her about his parents and their partying lifestyle, she bit her lip. *Would she be enough to keep him entertained?* Her pulse slowed and, stifling a yawn, she breathed out softly. She didn't have to be. This trip wasn't about partying and crowds. He wanted peace and birdsong. And *her*.

Or he would once he'd finished making his calls.

It was a comforting thought. Or it might have been had she not seen him sitting and staring out across the water, gaze unmoving, phone lying untouched next to where his fingers restlessly tapped the tabletop.

She tried to make sense of it. But after an hour her brain and body gave in to the heat of the day and finally, swiftly, she fell asleep.

CHAPTER SIX

IT WAS THE light falling across her face and a feeling of not quite knowing where she was that woke Addie. Somebody had closed the cream-coloured blinds, but she knew without even pulling them open that it was morning.

Her stomach flipped over nervously and she kept her eyes closed, basking in the soft whiteness of the morning, delaying the moment when she would have to face the man lying on the other side of the bed. What exactly was the correct way to greet your estranged husband the morning after the night before?

Her cheeks grew warm. Except there hadn't *been* a night before, because she'd fallen asleep instead.

She held her breath, wondering how he felt about that fact.

But there was only one way to find out and, gritting her teeth, she opened her eyes and rolled over.

Beside her the bed was empty. And not just empty. The sheet and pillowcase were perfectly smooth. Unless Malachi had slept several inches above the mattress, he hadn't slept there at all.

Her heart gave a twitch as she noticed a paper rose on the pillow beside her. Unfolding it, she saw that it was a note from Malachi, written in his familiar bold, cursive script.

Sweetheart,
I'm sorry I didn't wake you last night, only I thought you needed to sleep. I've got a couple of problems at work to sort out, but breakfast is all laid out so help yourself to what you want.
Terry is dropping round this morning, so if you need anything else ask him.
Malachi
PS—While I remember, the security pin is 2106. You'll need it to open any doors or windows. You shouldn't have a problem remembering it!

She read it again, and then twice more. Reading between every line, letter and punctuation mark. But the words stayed stubbornly the same, and finally she dropped the note onto the sheet beside her.

Of course she would remember the pin number. It was their wedding anniversary. Her mouth thinned. No doubt he'd chosen it to rub in the fact that this trip was a travesty of the honeymoon they might have had, had she not walked out on him. So much for the caring, sharing Malachi of last night.

Frowning, and suddenly feeling as restless as her thoughts, she pushed the sheet off. Rolling out of bed, she padded across the floor into the wet room.

As she stood under the warm spray of water, snippets of yesterday's lunchtime conversation with Malachi kept popping into her head, each one seeming to contradict the one before. It was so confusing. She couldn't seem to get a clear picture of what he'd said. It was almost as though she'd been talking to several different versions of the same man. But who was the *real* Malachi King? And how could she have been married to a man she knew so little about?

Then again, what did any of that matter now? He wasn't her concern any more.

Wrapped in a large fluffy towel, she walked back into the bedroom and gazed out of the window. It was another glorious day and it really was the perfect honeymoon location.

She lifted her chin. In another life, with another man, it might be, she told herself defiantly. But this was just a business trip. However, it was also probably going to be the only holiday she would ever spend on a private Caribbean island. So from now on she was going to make the most of every moment.

Selecting a new plum-coloured bikini, she covered it with a short crocheted dress—another recent purchase—and, pushing her feet into a pair of brightly coloured beaded sandals, did a twirl in front of the mirror. Glancing at her reflection, she gave a small, satisfied smile before turning and heading downstairs.

There was no sign of Malachi in the kitchen, but breakfast was indeed laid out on the wood-topped counter and, stomach rumbling, she picked out an almond croissant just as there was a knock at the front door.

Her first stupid thought was that it was Malachi.

But why would he knock at his own door? And then, remembering his note, she realised it must be Terry. Feeling suddenly shy, she walked hesitantly into the hallway and pulled down on the handle.

Nothing happened.

'Sorry, Miss Farrell...' Terry's voice floated through the door. 'You need the code.'

'Oh, yes, of course. I forgot,' she said, hastily punching her wedding date into the keypad and mentally cursing Malachi for his malicious choice of number.

Her irritation was forgotten, though, as she saw Terry's broad smiling face beaming down at her.

'Good morning, Miss Farrell! And how are you today?'

Taking his hand, she smiled back at him. 'I'm fine, Terry. Thank you.'

'I saw Mr King this morning and he told me to drop in and make sure you have everything you need.'

'I do—but while I remember, would you please thank Leonda for the wonderful food?'

Terry grinned. 'I will, Miss Farrell. She's real happy, having you and Mr King stay for all this time. Normally he's only here long enough to read the morning paper—which reminds me: Mr King asked me to drop off today's newspapers.' Reaching down, he picked up a bag. 'There's some magazines in there too. Let me put them inside for you, Miss Farrell.'

Inside the kitchen, he glanced out of the window and up at the sky.

'Weather's looking fine. We might even get some turtles next week.'

'There are *turtles*?' Addie said excitedly. 'Do they come into the lagoon?'

He shook his head again and laughed. 'No. Turtles like to nest near open water, so their babies can reach the ocean real quick.' As though sensing her disappointment, he smiled. 'But they *do* nest on Finlay's Island. You won't have seen it from the boat, but it's only thirty minutes away. I keep an eye out at this time of year, so I'll let you know if I see any sign of them. Now, is there anything else I can do?'

Addie nodded. An idea had just occurred to her. 'Actually,' she began tentatively, 'there *is* one thing…'

Ten minutes later, Addie was relaxing on a sun lounger, a glass of iced tea in her hand, thoroughly enjoying a celebrity gossip magazine. Having arranged for Terry to take them on a tour of the island, she felt calmer—more in control.

More like herself.

She took a sip of her tea. It wasn't that she didn't have a sexy side, but she wasn't comfortable about it being her defining quality. And now it wouldn't be.

A shadow fell across her face and her thought jammed inside her head as, looking up sharply, her eyes collided with Malachi's cool, assessing grey gaze.

'Good morning,' he said slowly, his eyes roaming over her in a way that made her whole body twitch restlessly.

Dressed in a pair of linen trousers and a navy polo shirt that clung to the muscular outline of his chest and arms, he looked relaxed and cool despite the heat of the morning.

'Morning!' Putting her glass down on the table beside her, she gave him what she hoped was a casual smile. 'I hope you don't mind, but I did have some breakfast.'

'Not at all.' He glanced back into the villa. 'I might just grab some fruit. Can I tempt you with anything else?'

'Like what?' Her eyes flicked up and he smiled at her mockingly.

'I meant some more iced tea, or something else to eat.'

Licking her lips, wondering how he managed to make such a mundane suggestion sound so enticing and decadent, she shook her head. 'No, thank you. I had a…thing…you know…' Her mind was suddenly a total blank, his proximity playing havoc with her brain. 'A pastry—almond—almond croissant,' she managed finally.

'Then I'll be right back!' he said softly, his clear, teasing gaze leaving her in no doubt that he knew the effect he was having on her.

Gritting her teeth, heart pounding, she watched his broad retreating back with a mixture of longing and relief. Moments later her breath seemed to punch out of her lungs as he dropped down lightly beside her on the lounger, the warm length of his thigh pressing against her naked leg.

'Why does everything taste so much better here than it does back on the mainland?' he murmured as he licked juice from his fingers. 'I know sugar's bad for you, but sometimes there's nothing better than that rush.' His eyes slid slowly over her face, fixing on her mouth. '*Almost* nothing anyway.'

Addie felt her stomach drop, and then a slow, prickling tension crept up her spine as he lowered his lips to hers and kissed her softly. Helplessly she arched against his body, feeling a quivering, featherlight pleasure steal over her skin, and then she breathed in sharply as Malachi lifted his head.

'Now, *that* is the correct way to say good morning!'

Staring down into Addie's dazed blue eyes, Malachi forced himself to blank off his mind to the clamouring of his body. His pulse was racing, and a fierce hot pressure was building in his groin. He had planned simply to kiss her, thereby reminding her of why she was sitting there, on *his* lounger, by *his* lagoon, looking so damn tempting. But now, with that red hair tumbling across her shoulders, her lips parted invitingly, it took every ounce of willpower he had not to scoop her up into his arms and take her right there and then.

Looking past her, he gritted his teeth, hating how stirred up she made him feel. He wanted her badly—so badly it felt like a toothache. But taking her now would only demonstrate that fact, and he'd arranged a little surprise for her that would be far more effective at enticing her into his arms.

He breathed out. Yesterday, after she had gone upstairs to lie down, he had fully intended to follow her. To give in finally to the hunger that had been growing inside him since the moment he'd heard her voice again.

Only he hadn't.

Oh, he'd wanted to. But he couldn't. His legs simply wouldn't move; it had been as if he was trapped inside his own body as once upon a time he'd been trapped as a unwilling onlooker at his parents' parties. How could he possibly have gone upstairs to Addie with that thought uppermost in his mind?

As for mentioning his parents to Addie—what had he been thinking? He shifted uncomfortably on the lounger. He'd worked so hard to suppress the hurt, to bury the memories. Now wasn't the time to let that darkness seep back into his life.

'Are you okay?' Looking up, he found Addie watching him warily.

He smiled, instantly back in control, and ran his fingers slowly down her arm, feeling her skin shiver beneath his touch. 'Of course. And you? Did you sleep okay?'

Her face stiffened. 'Yes. I did.' She hesitated. 'I'm sorry about falling asleep. I suppose I was more tired than I thought.' She frowned, not wanting to ask where he'd slept. Instead she said quickly. 'How did *you* sleep? Did you have a good night?'

It was not a night he would care to repeat, he thought grimly. And sleep had played a very small part in it. Having finally managed to clear his head enough to go and look for her, his erotic imaginings had turned increasingly feverish with every step, so that by the time he'd walked into the bedroom his body had been pulsing with desire.

Only of course she'd been fast asleep, her curled-up body seeming to emphasise her vulnerability and innocence. And, gazing down at her, he had cursed his timing. Waking a sleeping woman simply to gratify his sexual appetites was not something he could ever contemplate. But nor was lying next to *that* body when his mind was little more than a white-hot mass of sexually charged fantasies.

Which had left him tossing and twisting alone in a bed in one of the many spare rooms in the villa.

So, no. In answer to her question, he *hadn't* had a good night.

Or a particularly satisfying morning either. Having woken early and still painfully aroused, he had taken a long, cold shower, standing beneath the icy water until he simply couldn't feel his body any more. Stepping out of the shower, his libido once again checked and contained, he should have felt calmer.

His mouth thinned. Except that he hadn't. Instead he'd felt tense and on edge, his mind twitching with a whole set of new and unsettling feelings. Not least the realisation that Addie's presence appeared to be having an impact on more than just his libido. Staring down at where she lay in his bed, he'd felt more than thwarted lust. Maybe it had been the dark smudges beneath her eyes, or her slightly bitten fingernails, but something had twisted inside him and he'd felt a wholly uncharacteristic impulse to draw her into his arms.

He breathed out slowly. It didn't make any sense. But then what did in those strange early hours of the morning when the mind played tricks on itself? Once he'd finally bedded her he'd not only be free of this nagging physical ache but he'd also be able to think with his usual clear-headedness. After all, that was what sex did: it satisfied the body and soothed the mind.

He met her gaze. 'I always sleep well,' he lied, and watching her expression shift from curious to irritated, he felt a prickle of satisfaction.

That was more like it. Let her think she was a pleasurable diversion—not a compulsion that needed to be satisfied.

Feeling back in control, he stood up and, gazing out across the lagoon, he held out his hand. 'Come on! Let's go!'

Startled, Addie looked up at him. 'Go where?'

He grinned. 'To have a swim, of course.'

The lagoon was the perfect temperature and even though she was a fairly cautious swimmer, it would have been impossible for her not to enjoy herself. The warm water felt delicious on her skin, and everywhere there was something beautiful to look at. Tiny jewel-coloured fish. Shells of every shade of pink.

And Malachi.

Wearing nothing but a pair of navy trunks, his body was tugging at her gaze with the gravitational force of a black hole. She watched furtively as he pulled himself onto the deck, her eyes tracking the droplets of water trickling over his *café au lait* skin. He was shatteringly sexy.

Unfortunately at that moment he glanced over, and she felt her cheeks flame as she was caught in the act of watching him. Her breath faltered as he took a small run off the deck and dived back into the lagoon, cutting through the ripples towards her.

She stared at him dazedly, her brain melting. From a distance, his beauty was miraculous. Up close, it was as destabilising as an electromagnetic pulse and she could feel her resistance slipping away—

A shadow fell over her face at the same moment as a gust of air whipped up the water around them. Shocked, Addie gasped, her hand reaching out instinctively. Above them the unmistakable shadow of a helicopter hovered briefly, then swung away across the island.

'Don't worry!' Malachi's voice cut through the sudden silence that followed the helicopter's departure. 'They're just dropping something off for me.'

She nodded. At some point she had ended up clutching his arm and, mortified, she withdrew her hand swiftly, ignoring the mocking glint in his eyes.

'I might just go and get some sunblock. I don't want to burn on my first day.' Averting her eyes from his wet, muscular chest, she slipped past him and swam hastily across the lagoon and levered herself out onto the deck.

He was beside her in a moment, smoothing back his wet hair. 'Would you like me to put it on your back?' he said solicitously.

'No. It's fine. I probably should cover up now anyway.' Backing away, she grabbed her dress and tugged it hurriedly over her head as, behind them, the helicopter rose up above the trees and then swiftly disappeared from view.

Gazing after it, she suddenly remembered her plans for the day. 'Actually, I thought we could go and have a look round the island this morning,' she said quickly, inching towards the villa. Anything to get away from his fabulous semi-naked body. 'You know... Explore a bit.'

There was a short, tense silence. Looking up, she saw that he was watching her, his face as unyielding to her scrutiny as ever. But something was glittering in his eyes that made her heart jerk in her chest.

'Why would we want to do that?' he said softly. 'It's just more of the same.'

He paused and took a step closer, his gaze darkening in time with the beat of her heart. Reaching out, he ran his thumb along her collarbone and, hooking the front of her dress, he tugged her towards him.

'There are far more interesting places I'd like to explore right here.'

His hand was grazing her breast, caressing, circling, making her stomach muscles curl into a ball.

'Which reminds me—I have a little present for you.'

She followed him inside, watching warily as he walked across the kitchen to the counter and picked up a beautiful cream box tied with pale gold ribbon.

He handed it to her casually. 'This is for you.'

She swallowed, her breath hot and scratchy in her throat. Where had that box come from? She didn't remember seeing it earlier.

As though reading her mind, he fixed his eyes on her face. 'I arranged for the chopper to drop it off this morning.'

Gazing into his narrowed grey eyes, Addie felt her stomach flip over. Of course, she thought weakly. It

was just another example of the surreal, topsy-turvy
world in which he lived. Where his every whim was
magically and swiftly satisfied.

Trying not to think about how she fitted in with that
particular revelation, she glanced down at the box she
was holding. 'What is it?'

'Open it and see.'

Heart thudding, she tugged at the ribbon, struggling
to undo it. Finally she pulled off the lid and, parting
the feathery sheets of tissue paper, lifted out a short
silk slip. It was pale gold, trimmed with delicate cream
lace and utterly, utterly exquisite. She stared at it in silence, too stunned to speak.

'Do you like it?'

She nodded. 'It's beautiful, Malachi. I love the colour,' she said at last. Her cheeks grew warm. 'But I
don't have anything for you.' And what would she give
him anyway? she thought with a needle stab of pain.
The man who not only had everything but valued nothing except winning?

'Oh, I wouldn't say that,' he said slowly.

He lifted his gaze, locking on to her flushed, startled
face, and she felt a swirling liquid heat rise up inside
as his eyes roamed over her body with open longing.

'Try it on.'

His voice was soft, and had he been touching her
she might not have heard the authority beneath the seductive tone, for he wielded his body and her response
to it like a weapon, ruthlessly using every kiss, every
caress, to get what he wanted.

Only she must have wanted it too.

Or why else would she be hearing herself say, 'What? Here? Now?'?

His eyes met hers—dark, triumphant, like a runner who could see the finishing line.

He nodded slowly. 'Yes. Here. Now. Otherwise...' He paused, turning the word slowly over in his mouth, savouring it. 'How can I take it off?'

Something was wrong. *Yes. Here. Now.* His words were ringing inside her head like a series of off-key notes. But why? The slip was a present. A gift. A spontaneous gesture designed to give pleasure. Or was it? She had no reason to doubt him, but she couldn't shift the prickle of apprehension beneath her ribs. Why give her this today? Why not on the plane? Or yesterday?

Watching her in silence, his expression veiled, Malachi pictured her reaction, and inevitable surrender, feeling a rush of pre-emptive power. It was all part of the game. The game of seduction. And, like most games, it required nothing more than a cool head. And, of course, knowing when to make your move. It was a game he enjoyed playing. And winning.

Looking up, she found him studing her intently—and suddenly she knew why. His eyes had none of the heat or fire of a lover. Instead they were glittering down at her with a calculating coldness that made a shiver run down her spine.

She lifted her chin, her shoulders stiffening with suppressed anger. 'Why don't we wait until later?' she said coolly.

He frowned. 'Later?'

'Yes.' She met his gaze. 'You know I said I wanted

to explore the island? Well I arranged with Terry for him to give us a tour this morning.'

His eyes were suddenly harder than stone. 'So unarrange it,' he said arrogantly.

This time it was unequivocal. It was an order—clear and direct.

She glowered at him, her anger as quick and cold as a flash freeze. 'I will not.'

There was a long, pulsing silence.

Malachi stared at her, his disbelief that she had actually rebuffed him rapidly switching to cold, hard rage. This wasn't how it worked. Did she seriously think for one moment that *she* could set the agenda for this trip? Or that he was remotely interested in looking around the damn island with her? She was here for one reason and one reason only. Clearly now was the time to remind her of that fact.

'Then I will,' he said coldly. 'I don't know what fanciful little idea you've got in that pretty little head about why we're here, but let me make it easy for you to understand. It has *nothing* to do with sightseeing.'

A muscle flickered in his jaw. He could feel his control slipping and it did nothing to improve his temper. He had wanted to demonstrate his composure in the face of her helpless desire for him. Only instead he was acting like a thwarted teenage boy.

'And even if it did, the only sight I want to see is *you*. In *that*.' He gestured to the slip hanging from her hand.

'You're a monster,' she said shakily.

'And *you* are a hypocrite. Making all this fuss—'

His breath hissed through his teeth. 'We had an agreement. We still do.'

'I did *not* agree to this. To you snapping your fingers like some sexually depraved dictator.'

He shook his head. 'That's not what's happening here. You're just having a tantrum because I called you. In my house the rules are simple, sweetheart. Either fold or play.'

She stared at him in disbelief. Did he actually think this was like a game of cards?

'This is not a hand of poker.' She was practically shouting. 'This is you trampling all over my feelings.'

He shrugged. 'I don't care.'

It was his shrug as much as the cavalier tone in his voice that made something inside her snap. Her breath was suddenly choking her.

'Fine,' she snarled. 'Have it your way.'

Pulling her dress up over her head, she yanked off her bikini top, tugged the panties down from her hips and faced him—naked.

Malachi stared at her, his face hard with fury. 'What are you doing?'

'Me? Oh, I'm just getting ready for sex. That's why I'm here, isn't it?' Her voice was shaking, her breathing ragged. Dragging the slip over her head, careless of the delicate lace, she met his gaze. 'So where do you want to do it, then? On the table? On the beach?'

What was the matter with her? He shook his head, trying to control his anger, his confusion. 'You're being melodramatic!'

There was no reason for her to act like this. She'd

agreed to the deal. And the deal was about sex—not this raw emotion. So why was she making such a fuss?

She glared at him. 'No, I am not. I'm just being truthful. But honesty was never your strong point—was it, Malachi?'

'I never said you were just here for sex!' His voice was rough. He had finally lost his temper.

Swearing under his breath, he ran a trembling hand through his damp hair just as there was a knock on the door. He turned, frowning, and opened his mouth to say something. But Addie cut him off.

'Of course not. You never say what you mean to *anyone*! So why would today be any different?' Pressing her finger against her forehead, she pretended to think. 'Oh, I remember now. It's because I'm not just anyone. I'm your *wife*.'

'And I'm your husband. And you owe me a honeymoon and I always call in my debts.'

'You are *not* my husband. You're just a man who's blackmailing me for sex.'

He took a step towards her. The skin on his face was stretched tight; his arms were braced as though invisible hands were restraining him.

'If I'm blackmailing you, then how come *I'm* the one paying?'

She shook her head, her hands curling into fists. 'That's all you care about, isn't it? Money. And winning. I think you've lived and breathed that casino air for so long you think everything's like poker. That's why you're doing this. Why you've turned this, us, into some sort of sick fantasy game. You just can't help youself.'

Malachi stared at her in silence, his angry response stilled in his throat. He could *feel* her accusation, lodged beneath his skin like a poisoned dart. Hear it inside his head. Only it wasn't Addie's voice but his own, saying words he'd never had the courage to say out loud. Words he should have spoken long ago to people who should have known better. His head was spinning. This wasn't meant to be happening. He had just wanted to prove a point, but somehow he'd become the nightmare he'd been trying to escape from all his life.

He breathed in sharply, pushing aside that disturbing thought. 'It's not a game—' he began.

'Yes, it is,' she spat at him. 'Only you don't even know it. You actually think it's *normal* to manipulate your estranged wife into being your mistress. Or had it slipped your mind that we are still married?'

His eyes were hard and gleaming, like polished steel. 'I hadn't forgotten. But having not heard from you since your little outburst at our wedding reception, I'm surprised you bothered to bring it up.'

'Why should I contact you?' Her eyes flared with pain and anger. 'You lied to me.'

'I didn't lie,' he began. But she ignored him.

'And when I tried to talk to you about it you didn't want to know—'

'It was our *wedding*.' His face was as set as stone. 'Funnily enough I thought we might have other things on our mind. Like celebrating!'

'Celebrating what? The fact that you'd made a fool

out of me. Or rather I'd made a fool out of myself. And now I'm doing it again.'

She spat the words at him, wishing they weren't just words but bricks—something that would hurt him as he had hurt her. Was *still* hurting her.

'Calm down!' His eyes were glittering, their hostile glare fixed on her face. 'Terry might hear you.'

'And you wouldn't want *that*, would you, Malachi?' Her heart was thumping so hard she could hardly hear herself. 'You wouldn't want someone to actually hear what you're *really* like. How you use people. And exploit them. And hurt them.'

'Addie—' He started to speak but she shook her head.

'No. You've said enough.' She forced herself to meet his gaze. 'How can you think this is okay? Treating me like this? Like some whore?' The word stuck in her throat and suddenly she didn't care any more. Not about the deal she'd made with Malachi. Or the charity. Or Terry.

Blood roaring in her ears, she stared down at the slip sticking damply to her skin. She knew it was her body beneath the silk, but it didn't feel as if it belonged to her.

'You know, I thought nothing could ever feel as bad as when I found out I wouldn't be able to play the piano professionally.' It had been far worse five years ago, she thought dully. When she'd finally realised how ruthlessly Malachi had manipulated her love for him. The pain had felt like an actual wound.

How impossible it would have been then to imagine that she could sink any lower.

'It was like the end of everything.' Her voice trembled and she drew in a breath, pushing past the lump of misery in her throat. 'But I faced up to it. And I turned it into something good. Only you treating me like this—it's made me feel like I don't matter. That I'm nothing.'

It was true. She had never felt so utterly worthless. So tainted, so sordid.

'I don't even know who I am any more.' She swallowed, fighting to get her words out. 'I just know I don't like myself…this person I've become…' Her voice faltered and failed.

Malachi felt sick. He had known about her accident but he'd had no idea that it had robbed her of her dreams. She should have told him, he thought dully. Only why would she? Right from the start he'd made it clear that his past was off limits, and he'd never once encouraged her to talk about herself.

He stared at her in silence. She looked crushed, her face pale and trembling, her beautiful blue eyes clouded with pain. But it was her hands, clenched protectively in front of her, that made his body tense with shock.

He didn't like seeing her like that. He certainly didn't like knowing that he was responsible. The thought made him feel guilty, ashamed. He had turned their marriage into a game. He had trapped her and tried to manipulate her into doing what he wanted. He knew just how that felt, and yet he'd hurt her as he'd been hurt. His skin burned with shame.

'Addie—' Reaching out, he touched her hand gently, his heart twisting as she stiffened and shrank backwards.

'I can't do this,' she whispered.

With shock, he saw the sheen of tears in her eyes. He had never seen her cry and his throat felt tight. He didn't want to feel her pain. Didn't want to feel anything. But he had hurt her, and for the first time in a long, long time he wanted to face the pain. *Her* pain. Face it and erase it.

He took a step closer. 'Please listen to me, sweetheart.'

But, refusing to meet his gaze, she edged further away from his hand.

He stared at her uncertainly. What was he supposed to say? A cold, dull ache was seeping through his veins and he felt completely out of his depth. He'd spent most of his life avoiding scenes and confrontations, shunning anything remotely emotional, but as his eyes fixed on Addie's stricken face he felt his heart contract.

Suddenly his desires didn't seem all that important in comparison with comforting her. With helping her rebuild what he had so ruthlessly crushed.

He took a deep breath. 'I'm not a good person, Addie. I know that. But I swear it wasn't my intention to hurt you. And I can prove it to you if you let me. Please, Addie, let me make this right.'

'How can you?' she said flatly. 'Look what we're doing to each other. To our marriage. It's just so wrong—'

'It doesn't have to be like this.'

She heard him inhale and, looking up, saw that his eyes were fixed on her face, his expression strained.

'We can start over.'

For a moment she didn't reply and he held his breath, watching, waiting, until finally she lifted her head and sighed.

'I don't know what that means. But you'd better go and talk to Terry. I'm sure he's got better things to do than stand around on your doorstep.'

He nodded and walked swiftly into the hallway. She heard the door open and a muffled conversation. Moments later, the door closed and he returned.

'He's gone.' He met her gaze. 'Do you want me to go too?'

His face was set, and yet he seemed less self-assured than usual—as though he wasn't quite certain of her reply.

She gazed at him in silence. Was he playing with her? Or was he trying to make amends? Finally, she shook her head. 'No. I don't want you to go.''

He breathed out slowly. 'I meant what I said, sweetheart. About starting again.'

She watched in silence as, hesitantly, he reached out and touched her face.

'I want it to be good between us here.'

She bit her lip. 'Think about what's happening here, Malachi. I *sold* myself to you.'

Shaking his head, he stroked her cheek gently. 'Look at it this way: I can only afford you for a month.'

She gave him a tiny smile. 'Nice try! But I know a bluff when I hear one.'

'I'm not bluffing. You're a Royal Flush, sweetheart.'

He watched her face shift, the hurt showing through, and feeling a spasm of panic he reached out and grabbed her hands.

'I'm sorry. That was crass. I know you probably find this hard to believe, but not every thought I have is about poker.' He hesitated. 'Some are about you. Quite a lot, actually.' He felt her hands stiffen and, curling his fingers more tightly, he shook his head. 'I don't mean those kind of thoughts. I mean about *you*. The person you are.'

Addie stared at him in confusion. Was this really her uber-cool husband? He looked anything but cool. In fact he looked nervous, almost as though he didn't quite know what he was saying or doing.

She bit her lip. 'And who am I?'

His hands tightened around hers. 'You're a fighter. And a dreamer. Look at how you came back stronger after your accident.

'It stopped you from doing what you loved most but you didn't stop. You started a charity. Most people would have given up.'

Addie eyes him wearily. '*You* wouldn't.'

Her voice was quiet, but steadier, and he felt his heart lurch with hope. Maybe he hadn't ruined everything between them.

'No. It wouldn't have made me stronger. Or kinder.' But this wasn't about him. It was about Addie. 'I think you're one of the bravest people I know, sweetheart,' he said gently. 'And I'm really sorry for being such a jerk.' Tentatively, he slid his hand over her shoulder. 'Truly.

I know it's not enough, but it's a start, isn't it?' He breathed out slowly. 'Please, can we try again? Please?'

His eyes met hers and finally she nodded mutely.

He made as though to pull her against him and then, breathing out slowly, he turned and, reaching round, picked up her clothes from the floor. 'Here. Put these on.'

Averting his gaze, he waited until she was dressed and then slowly wrapped his arms around her and pulled her close.

'Thank you.' Gently, he kissed the top of her head. 'And now, how about we go and take a look around this island?'

CHAPTER SEVEN

'So—DO YOU have anything particular you'd like to do today?'

Leaning across the table to spear a piece of pineapple from a huge platter of fresh fruit, Malachi smiled at Addie. She held her breath. He was wearing a pair of dark blue swim shorts, and his long, muscular legs were sprawled out temptingly towards her. With his face tipped up to the sun and his dark hair falling loosely across his forehead, he looked impossibly glamorous, and intensely male, his lush beauty easily rivalling the tropical perfection surrounding them.

His eyes bumped into hers and he held her gaze so that she shifted restlessly in her chair. Her heart gave a twitch as he leaned forward, and for a moment she thought he was about to kiss her, but instead he picked up the coffeepot and topped up their cups.

'Actually, I do have something in mind. I just need to make a couple of calls.'

Picking up her cup, Addie wished that it was her hands and not the sunlight caressing his smooth golden skin. That she could reach over and loop her arm around his neck, press her hot, hopelessly overexcited body against his—

But wishing was all she was likely to do.

Skin prickling, she sipped her coffee. Yesterday she had felt so unhappy, so diminished by the way he was treating her. Only then they'd argued, and he'd pushed aside his obvious desire to comfort her, and his tenderness had shifted something inside her, opened her up to him. But now Malachi seemed to be on some kind of mission to prove that sex was the last thing on his mind. Oh, he kissed her, and curled his arm around her waist, but whenever she leaned into him, hoping, longing, wanting more, he merely let his hands drift over her back or arms.

Breathing out, she sat up straighter and forced herself to smile, hoping that her face appeared more composed than her body felt. 'Great. That sounds great.'

He stared at her thoughtfully. 'I haven't told you what it is yet.'

Her fingers spasmed involuntarily against the cup.

'I know,' she said quickly. 'But I'm sure it'll be great—whatever it is.'

Leaning forward, he grinned at her—a long, slow, curling smile that made her heart flutter in her chest and her breasts ache.

'How very trusting of you. Then I think I'll keep it as a surprise!'

An hour later she was regretting that trust as they skimmed across the water in the speedboat towards—who knew where?

'Can you please give me a clue?' Turning round, Addie gazed up in frustration at Malachi.

Grinning, he shook his head, his arm curving around her waist. 'I don't want to spoil the surprise,' he murmured, squeezing her hand.

She glanced up at him, her blue eyes wide and wary.

He laughed. 'Trust me, sweetheart. I know what you like and you're going to love this.'

His fingers lightly caressed her belly through the thin fabric of her dress, and eyes half closed, she feverishly imagined what she liked doing with Malachi, her skin quivering at the thought of the two of them moving slowly together, bodies entwined—

Her pulse gave a jolt and realising she needed to get a grip, she glanced past him to where a mass of greeny-brown was slowly growing larger. 'Is that Finlay Island? Is that where we're going?'

Smiling, he shook his head. 'Two more minutes and all will become clear.'

At that moment, the boat curved around the island and Addie felt her mouth fall open. 'Wh-what is *that*?'

He was watching her, gauging her reaction.

'That is the *Pearl Diver*. She's a submarine and my most recent acquisition. I thought you might like to join me on her maiden voyage.'

Too jolted to speak, Addie gazed in disbelief at where the submarine lay in the water. Finally she recovered and, looking up at him, she shook her head slowly. 'Let me guess! You're planning to build the world's first underwater casino.'

His eyes gleamed. 'Now, why didn't *I* think of that?'

Leaning forward, he ran a finger slowly under her chin, lifting her face to his. 'More importantly, why didn't my research and development team? Maybe I should give you a job there.'

She glanced at him sharply. Most likely he was joking. But then with Malachi it was impossible to know. Perhaps he thought he was offering her some kind of consolation prize.

Her stomach contracted at the thought of being downgraded from his wife to an employee but she managed to hold his gaze. 'Thanks, but I actually have a job I love.' She stared at the *Pearl Diver* and then back to Malachi, her curiosity piqued. 'So why did you buy a submarine?' She couldn't resist teasing him. 'Did all those other nasty billionaires have one before you?'

The corners of his mouth tugged upwards. 'Well, now you come to mention it—'

She shook her head. 'You're impossible!'

His grey eyes searched her face and suddenly she was holding her breath. Finally, when she thought her lungs might burst, he shrugged.

'I just thought that as you liked exploring the island so much, you might want to take a look around under the water.'

'You did?'

Knots were forming in her stomach. Was that true? Had he really arranged this trip for *her*? Trying not to read anything into his words, she swallowed down the bubble of happiness rising in her throat and gave him a small, uncertain smile.

He smiled back at her. 'You seem a little surprised.'

'Yes—I mean, no!' She bit her lip. 'It's just that I didn't—you don't—I thought—' She took a breath. 'That's very considerate of you,' she finished, her voice trailing off as he stared at her assessingly, his gaze seeming to reach inside her in a way that made her nerves dance into life.

'Considerate…' Fingers tightening around hers, he turned the word over in his mouth as though tasting it. 'Is that what I am? And there I was, thinking I was being romantic.' He spoke teasingly but there was an intensity to his expression she didn't understand.

Addie felt her face still. Romantic! Once that had been her dream. And for a short time she had even believed it was possible. That Malachi was capable of loving her and of expressing that love. Now, with his hair falling across his forehead and those smoky eyes fixed on her face, it was tempting to believe there was some truth behind his teasing words. But of course there wasn't. Her face tightened. No matter how poetic his language the only hearts he was interested in were those on the front of playing cards.

She lifted her chin. 'I would swoon, only it's difficult when you're sitting down.'

His eyes narrowed, or maybe it was the sunlight playing tricks, for the next moment his face was smooth and untroubled and smiling. He said slowly, 'I'll just have to think of another way to sweep you off your feet.'

For a moment she could think of nothing to say. Could think only of how it felt to be the focus of his attention. To feel his smile and hear his laughter. It was like the summer sun after a stormy spring.

She took a quick breath. *Now who was being poetic?*

Poetry was far from her mind twenty minutes later as she stood in the bedroom of the submarine's master suite. Instead, as a dizzying heat surged over her skin, she found herself thinking of the mind-blowing number of ways that she and Malachi could amuse themselves on a bed like that.

Feeling her insides tighten, she squeezed her thighs together, the muffled thud of her heart suddenly competing with the rhythmic throb of the engine.

'You're shaking.' Malachi looked down at her, frowning. 'Are you okay?'

'I'm fine.' Looking up, she gave him a quick, tight smile. 'It's probably too much adrenaline. I can't believe this is happening. That I'm in an actual submarine. It doesn't feel real.'

Malachi stared down at her face. Her cheeks were flushed and her eyes dazed, and he felt his groin tighten. Almost half his life had been spent chasing the next thrill, the biggest risk, pushing boundaries— breaking rules. Yet nothing he'd done had felt as intoxicating as seeing her naked, unguarded excitement. Or knowing that he had made her feel like that.

His body stilled. A prickling heat was crawling over his skin. There was nothing between them but her dress and his shirt and shorts. He wanted her more than he had ever desired any woman *and she wanted him*. But he held himself back; it would happen…but when it did the time would be of her choosing.

'Oh, it's real, all right,' he said lightly. Loosening his grip, he held out his hand. 'Here. Let me prove it to you.'

Addie felt her stomach flip over as, handing her a small black remote control, he gave her one of his devastating smiles.

'See that button in the middle? The blue one? Press that.'

She pressed it. For a moment nothing happened, and then there was a whirring noise and the walls of the cabin started to move. Or rather they weren't walls, she saw now, but huge blinds. As they rolled slowly upwards she took a step backwards, her mouth dropping open.

On the other side of the window was the bluest blue she had ever seen. Only it wasn't just blue. It was white and gold and green and red. Stepping forward, she reached out and touched the glass with a hand that shook slightly. She had never seen colours like that. The coral was like a living rainbow. And everywhere there were fish of every shade and shape.

'What do you think?' Malachi was standing behind her.

She turned and shook her head. 'It's like another world,' she whispered.

'It's our world!'

His arm brushed against her body as he pointed past her and through the glass. 'See over there? That's the wreck of the *Creole Queen*. The Captain came across her last month. She's a three-master, sunk during a storm in 1785.' He paused, his eyes roaming over her face. 'If you like, we could go and check her out. You never know—we might find some treasure.'

She looked up at him, her eyes wide. 'Is that possible?'

He grinned. 'I can't see why not. There are hundreds of wrecks out here. The odds are that some of them must have something of value on board.'

She nodded. 'That's true, I suppose.' She looked up at him and smiled, wanting to tease. 'But what happens if we do find some treasure? How do I know you won't steal my share?'

'How do I know you won't steal mine?' Slowly he ran a finger down her arm, making it impossible for her to concentrate.

She swallowed. 'You don't.'

For a moment she held her breath, mesmerised, as he stared at her thoughtfully, his face giving nothing away, his eyes revealing even less. Then slowly he smiled.

'In that case I don't think we have any alternative. We're just going to have to keep a very close eye on one another.'

The dive was incredible. Addie had only ever snorkelled before, but Malachi was an experienced scuba diver and a surprisingly patient teacher. Afterwards they ate a leisurely lunch on a secluded beach on another island chosen by the captain, and it was then that a wave of tiredness hit her head-on.

'I feel shattered,' she said, stifling a yawn as they headed back to the submarine. 'Is that normal?'

Malachi grinned. 'Completely. First dives always take it out of you.'

She sighed. 'I think I might just have a little lie-down. What are you going to do?'

His eyes gleamed. 'I'm going to have a little play at being a submarine captain, but I promise I'll wake you in a bit.'

After he'd left, Addie took a shower and then lay down on the bed, closing her eyes with relief. Letting the soporific hum of the engine wash over her, she breathed out softly…

Waking some time later, she picked up her phone and stared groggily at the screen, frowning as she saw the time. She had slept for three hours! Sitting up, she pushed back the sheet—and then her eyes widened. Lying across the covers at the end of the bed was the most beautiful dress she had ever seen. It was full-length and blue, the same blue as the centre of a flame, and beside it was a pair of slightly darker high-heeled court shoes.

Heart pounding, she scrambled off the bed and picked up the dress. Slipping it over her head, she zipped herself up. It was cut into a deep V at the front, and the slit running up the side practically reached her pelvic bone. But it felt divine on, like a second silken skin. Grabbing hold of the wardrobe to steady herself, she pushed her feet into the shoes then turning, she took a step forward and stared at herself in the full-length mirror.

Was that really her? It took her several nervous glances to accept that it was. The dress fitted beautifully, but...

She glanced doubtfully down at her plunging cleavage.

'No, it's not.'

Her head snapped up, her body tightening automatically at the sound of Malachi's voice. Rooted to the floor, gripped by equal amounts of fear and longing, she stared helplessly at his reflection in the mirror. He was standing behind her in the doorway, wearing a beautifully cut dinner jacket, his white shirt unbuttoned at the neck, a bow tie hanging loose around the collar. In one hand he was holding a bottle of champagne, in the other a pair of long-stemmed glasses. He looked impossibly sexy and irresistibly glamorous.

'It's not too low. That's what you were thinking, wasn't it?'

She nodded, suddenly too shy to speak. He walked towards her slowly and her heart gave a jolt as he reached out and gently slid his palm around her waist, forcing her to face him.

His face was serious, his eyes dark and focused. 'You look beautiful, sweetheart. Far too beautiful for a two-bit hustler like me! And that dress fits you to perfection.'

She swallowed, trying to play it cool. 'Thank you. And thank you for getting it for me. But how did you know my size?'

He smiled—a sexy, curling smile that made her

heart pound so hard she thought it would burst through her chest.

'It wasn't hard,' he said softly. 'I've been giving your body an awful lot of thought over the last few days.'

There was a tense, pulsing silence. Addie gazed up at him helplessly, the softness of his voice as much as the implication in his words playing havoc with her nerves.

Finally she managed to pull herself together. 'You did a good job. And you look amazing too,' she said hoarsely. 'I love that you haven't done up your tie.'

He grinned. 'I'd *love* to pretend it was a conscious fashion choice, but sadly it's just down to my incompetence. I did, however, manage to lay my hands on a bottle of champagne, so hopefully you won't spend the entire evening wondering how you got stuck with a loser like me!'

A loser! Addie gazed at him. She doubted Malachi had lost at anything—ever. She, on the other hand, would lose all self-control if they didn't leave the bedroom soon.

'Here!' He held out the glasses and, popping the cork, he poured the champagne. 'To the high seas! And sunken treasure.' He tapped his glass lightly against hers. 'Now, let's eat. I am *starving*.'

The meal was delicious: a starter of burrata salad followed by *taglierini* with shaved white truffles and a chocolate fondant for dessert.

'I'm so glad it's not fish,' Addie said, glancing out of the window at the darkened ocean. 'What if they'd looked in and seen us?'

Malachi grinned. He had taken off his jacket and his tanned muscular skin was perfectly offset by the pure white of his shirt.

'I think they'd be pleased you weren't eating *them*. It's a fish-eat-fish world out there.'

Laughing, she pushed away her empty bowl and took a sip from her wine glass.

'What are you thinking?'

'Nothing really!' Turning her head, she saw he was watching her, his face in the candlelight somehow softer, less guarded. 'Just how much the children would love this. You don't mind if I show them a photo or two, do you?' She gave him a small, tight smile. 'Otherwise they might not believe me.'

He shook his head, frowning slightly. 'No, of course not.'

'Thank you.' The easy atmosphere of moments earlier seemed to have disappeared. Confused, suddenly on edge herself, she lifted her chin. 'Sorry to bring up work. It just popped into my head.'

There was a short, strained silence.

'It's not just work, though, is it? For you, I mean.'

She looked up at him, startled. He was looking at her, his expression an odd blend of curiosity and appraisal.

'You really care about those children.'

'Yes. I do.' She was shocked at how fierce she sounded. 'They deserve it. Some of them—a lot of them—have such difficult lives, and they're so brave.'

'They're lucky to have you championing them.' He

held her gaze. 'I can't think of many people I'd rather have by my side, watching my back.'

She held her breath. Then why had he pushed her away? She'd been by *his* side, watching *his* back. When all the time she should have been watching her own.

She shrugged. 'I'm not a saint. I get a lot back from them.'

Malachi stared at her. In that dress it would be difficult for any woman to look like a saint. He wondered if she had any idea how beautiful she was. How sexy. He wanted her so much. But for the first time in his life sex didn't seem that important. Not as important as hearing her story.

'Like what?' Leaning forward, he topped up her glass, then his.

Her face softened. 'Like having fun. And a purpose. After my accident I couldn't imagine doing anything with music. It hurt just thinking about what I'd lost. I was so miserable.

'So what changed?' His hand tightened around his glass. He hated the idea of her being that unhappy almost as much as he hated himself for not having known about it before.

'I did this workshop in a school and I realised that music isn't only about that one perfect solo performance. It's about sharing and creating.' She frowned. 'That's when I accepted that I wasn't going to have the life I'd planned. But I was going to have a life that *mattered*.' Meeting his gaze, she smiled weakly. 'Or at least one that wasn't as boring and lonely as lying in a hospital bed for weeks and weeks.'

He was staring at her intently and she fell silent. Malachi was unlikely to be familiar with the concepts of boredom and loneliness, let alone understand them. But after a short, stilted pause, he nodded slowly.

'That's why I started playing cards. Boredom.' He shifted, staring past her, his eyes suddenly cloudy. 'I must have been about seven. We were in Europe, visiting friends of my parents'.'

Abruptly he picked up his glass and drained his wine.

'I was always the only child, and my parents liked to party hard. Often they didn't surface until the afternoon, and I used to get so bored and then one day one of the valets at the hotel where we were staying taught me how to play patience. Then blackjack and then poker.'

His face tightened.

'I got real good, real quick.' He gave her a small, taut smile. That's the upside of living in hotels—there's always a bunch of people going on and off shift and a lot of them play cards.

Addie stared at him, trying to fit his words into the image of the Malachi she knew.

'I thought your dad must have taught you,' she said slowly.

He shook his head. 'No. He taught me other things, but I think those will keep for another day. Shall we have coffee?'

She said nothing, but her mind was buzzing with questions. Why had they never talked about his childhood before? And why were so many subjects off limits? Was it something to do with his father? Had they argued? Was that why his parents hadn't come to their wedding?

Pushing his chair back, Malachi stood and held out his hand.

Coffee was waiting for them in the lounge area.

Addie took a sip and frowned. 'What is that flavour?'

'Cardamom. If you don't like it I can get them to bring some different coffee.'

She shook her head. 'No, I like it. It's kind of spicy.' His eyes narrowed and she felt her stomach clench. 'M-maybe not spicy,' she stammered. 'More…hot without the heat.'

His gaze locked on to hers and she felt a shiver run down her spine as he reached out and ran his hand up and down her arm, grazing her breast with his knuckles.

'Hot without the heat? Sounds interesting.'

Heart pounding, she forced herself to meet his gaze. 'I'm talking rubbish. And I haven't even had that much wine. It must be all that oxygen earlier. I'll probably be seeing mermaids next.'

His hand stopped moving. It felt warm and steady on her arm, matching the warmth and steadiness of his gaze.

'I'm already seeing them. Or one, at least.'

Her breath felt suddenly thick and hot in her throat. 'It's just the dress…' she said hoarsely.

'No. It's this as well.' Gently he slid his hand up

into her hair, threading it through his fingers. 'And these...'

Tilting his head, he brushed his lips across hers gently, so that her head was swimming.

'You've bewitched me,' he murmured and, lowering his mouth, kissed her again more deeply.

It was the closest he would get to expressing any feelings of tenderness.

'So how come I'm at the bottom of the ocean in your submarine?' she whispered.

He smiled—a long, slow, curling smile that made her stomach disappear. 'Do you want me to take you back up to the surface?'

His eyes were huge and dark above her face, so that she felt as though she were drowning in them.

Slowly she shook her head. 'I want to stay down here for ever.'

'That could be arranged.' His voice was hoarse, his eyes burning into hers.

She stared up at him unsteadily. 'Wouldn't we run out of air?' she asked. She felt his fingertips graze her collarbone and slide slowly under the chin, lifting her face.

'Eventually. But we'd use it up slower if we shared.'

Her pulse was racing. 'How do you share air?'

'It's easy,' he murmured. 'You just do this.'

And, lowering his mouth again, he kissed her. She gasped, her lips parting, heat flooding her body. Clutching on to his arm, she felt her pulse jerk as his tongue probed her mouth. Heat, sharp and raw, flared up inside her, and suddenly her fingers were pulling at his shirt, tugging clumsily at the buttons.

Tangling her hands through his hair, she kissed him fiercely, pressing against the hard muscles of his naked chest. She felt him respond, deepening the kiss, his hand sliding around her waist, pulling her up against him. It felt so, so good. So right. No other man could make her feel this way. Only Malachi.

He broke the kiss. 'Are you sure?'

His face was tight with concentration, his arms shaking with tension and desire. The raw need in his voice reached inside her. Heart thudding, Addie breathed in shakily. Her eyes lifted and locked on to his and she saw that he was holding himself back, his muscles straining, his longing spilling over her skin like molten lava.

Dry-mouthed, Malachi held his breath. The last few days and nights his mind had been tormented by erotic images of Addie, but none had come close to how mind-blowingly sexy she looked right now. With her long red hair tangling around her shoulders, that incredible blue dress clinging to every curve like a second skin.

For a moment she stared at him, her eyes narrow blue slits, and then she nodded slowly and he felt his self-control slip away.

Pulling her to her feet, he scooped her into his arms. The blood was pulsing in his head. She was so soft in his arms, her body curving against his in obedient response to the heat of his lips and the touch of his hands. Striding across the floor, he pushed open the door to the bedroom and, kicking it shut, let her feet drop to the floor.

His fingers threaded through her hair, twisting and tugging it up from the nape of her neck. Whole body shaking, he pulled her against him, the sweet taste of her mouth tearing at his senses, and then he was walking her backwards, nudging her with his body, his knuckles scraping against the wall as they banged against it.

Lowering his lips, he licked her throat, tasting the salt on her skin as he grabbed her arms, stretching them high above her head, trapping her wrists with one hand, sliding the other down over her throat to her breast, his fingertips pushing beneath the satin, brushing lightly against a nipple.

Addie shuddered, her body straining helplessly against his, her belly hot and tight, and then she was arching upwards, whimpering, her fingers splaying apart as his mouth closed over her nipple, sucking the swollen tip.

Hearing her soft moan, Malachi nearly lost it. Groaning, lifting his mouth, he dropped her wrists and stepped back unsteadily.

For a moment he stared at her in silence, his breathing ragged, his gaze dark and fixed. Then slowly he reached out and touched her throat, running his hand lightly over her collarbone. With his other hand he reached for her zip and the heavy satin slid to the floor.

Malachi felt his whole body stiffen. She was naked except for a barely-there pair of panties. Looking at her, he could barely breathe. His blood was humming in his veins and then he was jerking her up against him, pushing her back against the wall. His whole body seemed to explode in a fireball of heat as he felt her hand tug at his belt, tearing the zip down, her fingers pulling the hard length of him free.

'Addie—'

Breathing in sharply, he felt her hand tighten around him, so that his body seemed to stretch out. His muscles started to spasm as he reached between her thighs, pushing aside the scrap of lace and opening her legs wider, dipping his fingers into the warm, slick heat.

Panting, eyes widening, Addie caught his hand, jerking it away. She guided him towards her, her body jolting up to meet his as he lifted her easily and thrust inside. Instantly she was lost, drowning in a shuddering, sensual heat. Eyes closed, she pressed against him, raising her hips as his fingers curled beneath her.

Tightening his grip, he pushed deeper still, opening her, stretching her. She bowed her back, meeting his thrusts, her nails digging into his shoulders, her breath quickening in time to the pulse clamouring between her thighs and then, shuddering, he groaned. And as she felt him spill inside her, her body convulsed around his.

Burying her head against the hollow of his shoulder, Addie breathed out unsteadily, letting her body go limp in his arms. She could feel his heart pounding, his skin damp against hers. Finally he shifted, gently withdrawing, and she felt his lips brush her hair. Somehow he got her onto the bed and she lay curled against his chest, his body damp and warm beneath her.

Staring down at her flushed face, Malachi grimaced. 'I didn't hurt you, did I?' He hesitated and then pulled her into his arms, pressing his face into her hair. 'I tried to stop but I just couldn't. I wanted you so badly.'

He had never felt that desperate. His breathing raw and uneven, he lifted his head, wanting, needing to see her face.

'I don't know what happens when I'm with you.'

She gazed up at him, stunned, mute, muscles aching. He looked as dazed as she felt. And was he really admitting that he'd just lost control?

She wanted to hear more—wanted to ask him what he meant—but she could hardly think straight, let alone speak. But it didn't matter, she thought, her eyes closing as she leaned into him. Just for the moment, nothing mattered except him and her and the beating of their hearts…

CHAPTER EIGHT

FINALLY! AN *ACE*. Feeling a twinge of satisfaction, Malachi placed the card on the table in front of him. Behind him, he heard Addie shift in her sleep and, glancing back at the bed, felt his breath catch in his throat. With her red hair gleaming in the silvery light flooding the bedroom she looked even more like a mermaid than ever.

For a moment he watched her sleep then, breathing out slowly, turned back to his cards. Addie might be sleeping soundly, but sadly he was not. And he couldn't quite work out why.

After she had got so upset, he had played it slow, choosing to wait, savouring the intensity and heat of his longing so that his desire had been raw and fierce. He had never wanted any woman as much as he had wanted her in that moment. Never waited so long for any woman. But it had definitely been worth the wait.

He should be feeling sated, satisfied. And yet here he was, wide awake, body twitching with lust, playing cards by himself in the moonlight.

It didn't make any sense. Sex was supposed to solve

problems. Not create them. In his head, tapping into their passion had seemed like a foolproof solution to the niggling problem of the sexual hold she appeared to have over him. Only his plan didn't seem to be working out. Rather than killing his desire, having sex with her not only seemed to have heightened his libido but it seemed to be messing with his mind.

Take earlier. Usually, post-coital affection was something to be avoided, at best endured. But he had found it impossible to lie next to her and *not* hold her close. He'd actually had to get out of bed to stop himself from doing so.

Standing up, he walked softly across the room and stared down at Addie in silence. For the first time in his life sex didn't seem to be an end in itself. Instead it felt more like a means to an end.

He breathed out slowly. Something was happening. He was feeling things he hadn't expected or wanted to feel. Like the fact that this deal with Addie no longer seemed that important. Instead what mattered was spending time with her. Which was why he was going to take her with him to Venezuela, for the opening of his newest casino.

In the bed, Addie shifted onto her side, and then her eyelids fluttered open and she looked up at him drowsily. 'What's the matter?'

Gently he stroked her face. 'Nothing. I'm just not that sleepy.'

She smiled, her lips parting. 'Me neither.'

His eyes fixed on her face and there was a short beat of silence and then, sliding beneath the sheet, he pulled her soft, unresisting body against his and, capturing her mouth, kissed her fiercely.

'I'll have your twos, please!' Biting her lip nervously, Addie peered over the top of her sunglasses to where Malachi lay sprawled on the other side of the huge bean-filled lounger.

For a moment he stared impassively at his cards, and then finally he sighed and a wicked smile spread slowly over his face. 'Go fish! And I'll have *your* threes, please, sweetheart.'

'You are such a rat!' Shaking her head, she dropped her cards into his outstretched hand and picked up another from the deck.

Two minutes later it was all over.

Groaning, Addie rolled over onto her back. 'I can't believe I lost. *Again.* I thought you said you'd never played go fish before?' she said accusingly.

Shuffling the cards with the skill of a Vegas croupier, Malachi grinned. 'I haven't. Is that why you wanted me to play with you?' His eyes were watching her with amusement. 'So you could take advantage of me.'

Addie laughed. 'It did cross my mind.'

'It did, did it?' Reaching out, he grabbed hold of her hand and pulled her towards him, pinning her against the cushion with his thigh and his hand. 'Then maybe I should reciprocate.'

Her breath caught in her throat as he picked up a handful of glossy red hair, threading it through his fingers.

'Take advantage of *you* in some way.'

She stared up at him, tilting her head back to watch the play of sunlight on his face.

It had been a strange and strained few days. But Malachi seemed different now. Calmer...more relaxed. As though some tension had been eased. But then, she felt the same way too, so maybe it was just down to the two of them getting used to being around one another again.

Only it felt as if there was more to it than just the pair of them getting reacquainted. Her heart began to pound as she remembered how he had comforted her when she'd got upset. It was so out of character for him; he hated scenes, and yet he had shelved his obvious and pressing desire and let her talk—asking questions, listening to her answers.

Addie breathed out slowly. It was all so confusing. Almost as confusing as her feelings for Malachi.

She shouldn't really be enjoying herself. And yet if she just concentrated on living in the moment then the truth was that she had never been happier. *Not even when they were engaged and she'd thought Malachi actually loved her.*

She felt his gaze on her face and, pushing aside her thoughts, reached out and looped her arms around his neck. 'What do you have in mind?' she said softly.

'I'm not entirely sure,' he murmured and, shifting forward, he covered her mouth with his and abruptly all conscious thought was driven from her head.

Later, body aching, she lay curled against him, her fingers tracing the muscles of his stomach.

'So why are you opening a casino in Caracas, then?' Tipping her head back, Addie stared up at him curiously.

Frowning, Malachi shrugged. 'No reason other than I've been looking to expand into South America for a couple of years now.'

She nodded politely, barely listening. Her head was still reeling from the fact that he had asked her to go with him, and she wondered how this very public event fitted into their deal. Here, on this island, their relationship might be unorthodox but it was private. However, he could hardly parade her around as his mistress at some huge, social event.

Her heart skipped a beat.

But why did it matter? It wasn't as if she cared.

The answer to her question popped into her head, unwelcome and unwanted like a bill through a letter box. *Of course she cared. Not just about their relationship but about him.*

She breathed out slowly. It wasn't that much of a shock, but still—

It was strange, but even now, five years after they had separated, there was still this connection between them. Some sense of being more than married. It might not make any sense, and ultimately it didn't change anything, but that didn't stop it being the reason why she had never divorced him. Or why a tiny part of her wanted to stop being his mistress and go to Caracas as his *wife*.

His voice bumped into her thoughts and she stared

up at him, trying to pick up the thread of their conversation.

'Sorry—I was…' She paused. 'It's just—are you sure you want me to be there?'

He stared at her thoughtfully. 'Of course.' His eyes were cool. 'I want to get my money's worth.'

There was a short, stilted silence, and then they both jumped as Malachi's phone rang.

Retrieving it from his pocket, he glanced momentarily at the screen and then answered it. 'Yes—no—I highly doubt that.'

Face blank, he shifted away from her, the muscles of his stomach suddenly taut and strained beneath her fingers, and after a moment of indecision she withdrew her hand. He stood and turned and, watching his shoulders tighten, she wondered who was on the other end of the phone. His voice was quiet, but she could hear a tension that hadn't been there before. With shock, she realised that he was struggling to maintain his composure.

Feeling as though she was intruding, she reached out and picked up a handful of sand, letting it run through her fingers.

Behind her, Malachi was winding up the call. 'Okay, that's fine. Just leave it to me. I'll sort it out.' He hung up.

Heart thudding, Addie stared at the back of his head, trying and failing to work out what had just happened.

'Is everything okay?' she said finally.

She was being polite. Clearly it wasn't okay—at

least not if the prickly energy coming off him was anything to go by.

But when he turned he simply smiled at her. 'Everything's fine. It's nothing.'

She nodded mutely. It was the same smile he'd used when he was playing cards with her earlier. The one that was impossible to read. Probably it was the smile he used every day with anyone he wanted to keep at arm's length. She felt a stab of misery. The easy warmth between them had trickled away just like the sand between her fingers.

Slowly, she stood up. She could just leave it. He'd told her it was nothing, and even if it wasn't it was none of her concern. But there was something in that smile. Something in that voice that made her heart contract. And even though it was pointless to do so, she still cared about him. Still cared that he was hurting and upset.

She took a deep breath. 'Is it work?'

He stared at her. He was still smiling, but his eyes were the cool grey of a battleship.

'No. Work looks after itself. My parents, on the other hand, need a team of full-time minders.'

'Your parents?' Her pulse jerked. 'What's happened? Are they okay?'

He gave a casual shrug. 'I expect so. It's happened before. I'm sure it's fixable.'

He paused and she watched his expression shift and clear, like one of those drawing toys where with one shake the picture disappeared.

'But—' she began.

'Don't worry about it.' He interrupted her. 'It's nothing, I promise. It certainly won't take more than a couple of hours to sort out. And thankfully they're only in Miami. The last time this happened they were in Cannes.'

Addie gazed at him in confusion. 'Are you saying we're going back to Miami?' she said hesitantly.

He looked at her in disbelief. 'No. There's absolutely no reason for you to be dragged into any of this. I'll go on my own. If I take the helicopter and leave now I'll be back this evening. Tomorrow morning at the latest.'

'But—' She frowned. 'Surely it would be better if I came with you.'

'Better?' he repeated. 'In what way would it be better?'

'I don't know. I just thought you might like to have a bit of support. Maybe I can help—'

'You want to help me with my parents?' Shaking his head, he laughed harshly. 'I see. I should warn you they're both tone deaf, so they might not be that responsive to music therapy.'

Addie stared at him, her breath hot in her throat, anger balling in her chest. It was like talking to a stranger, she thought wildly. A handsome, detached stranger. Instead of the man she had let inside her body.

'I don't understand,' she said slowly.

His face didn't alter but his eyes narrowed fractionally. 'You don't need to. This is *way* beyond your pay grade, sweetheart.'

She stared at him in silence, breathing unsteadily.

Her whole body was suddenly trembling with anger. 'Is that right?' she said icily. 'Then maybe I should ask for a raise, because you're certainly not paying me enough to put up with *that* kind of remark.'

His face stiffened. 'You're overreacting,' he said softly. 'As I said before, there's no need for you to come to Miami with me.' His eyes met hers. 'If you really want to help, stay here—and then we can go to Caracas together as planned.'

'So you want me to come to Caracas but you don't want me to meet your parents—' She broke off, suddenly too angry and frustrated and upset to speak. 'If you're so ashamed of me, then maybe I shouldn't be here in the first place.'

He frowned, his face darkening. 'I'm not ashamed of you.'

'Then what's the problem?'

'There *is* no problem. Except you. You're making it a problem.'

'How? By wanting to meet your parents?'

'This—us—it has nothing to do with them.'

'Is that why they didn't come to our wedding?'

The words were out of her mouth before she could stop them. The question he had refused to answer five years ago. His parents' absence at their wedding had always mattered to her. But now she knew that it had mattered to Malachi too, for she felt the change in him even before she saw it in his eyes.

'They didn't come because I didn't ask them.' His voice echoed harshly between them. 'You wouldn't understand. But then I'm not asking you to.'

'But you *are* asking me to go and watch you open your new casino?'

He stared at her. 'Please try and be reasonable, sweetheart. The two aren't in any way connected—'

'If you say so,' she snapped. 'Just go, Malachi.' Picking up her towel, she stalked past him. 'I'm going for a swim. Have a nice trip.'

Wading into the lagoon, she stared fixedly ahead, too furious even to register her beautiful surroundings. But the water felt cool against her skin, and the soft breeze and faint scent of frangipani was soothing, and slowly her anger started to fade.

Malachi was impossible. Rude and secretive and— '*"Please try and be reasonable, sweetheart!"*' she muttered.

It wasn't the most convincing impression of him, but it made her feel better, and suddenly determined not to let him spoil everything she began to swim with strong, firm strokes. Ten minutes later, smoothing the damp strands of hair away from her face, she glanced back at the beach, frowning. She was sure she had left her towel just under that palm tree...

And then her pulse gave a jolt as she saw Malachi standing at the edge of the sand, the towel in his hand.

Her footsteps faltered but then, lifting her chin, she marched towards him.

'Aren't you supposed to be on your way to Miami?' she snapped.

He didn't reply, just held out his hand. Pulse quickening, she stared at him warily.

'I know it looks like a towel,' he said quietly. 'But it's actually an olive branch.'

She didn't reply.

Malachi watched her face shift, saw her swallow and breathe in sharply. He could see the conflict in her eyes; the longing to believe his words, the hurt holding her back.

He was on the verge of trying again when abruptly she looked up at him and said, 'What do you want, Malachi?'

He cleared his throat. 'I want you to come with me. To Miami. If you still want to, that is.'

She held his gaze. Her blue eyes were no longer glazed and drowsy, as they had been earlier, after they'd made love on the beach, but dark and stormy. And hostile. Very, *very* hostile.

'I thought that was above my pay grade.'

Sighing, Malachi ran a hand over his face. His head was pounding, his stomach knotted with tension. Watching her walk away, he had felt a savage and unreasonable anger. Anger with his parents for messing up his time in paradise, anger with himself for letting his guard down. And anger with Addie for—

For what? For wanting to help him? For caring?

Picturing her face, he had felt his rage give way to shock as he'd realised what he'd seen but chosen to ignore. That she was worried about him. That she cared.

'I shouldn't have said that. It was rude and I'm sorry. It's just that I never— I haven't—' He stopped. Things were getting so complicated. How much should he say? There was so much she wouldn't understand.

She took the towel from his hand. 'I know,' she said quietly. 'I do know what it's like to have things inside your head you don't want to share. After my accident I got sick of people asking me what I was thinking. You don't have to tell me everything. Or anything. Not if you don't want to. I just didn't want you to have to deal with whatever it is on your own.'

He stared at her. 'Then come with me. That way I won't need to tell you. You'll be able to see it for yourself.'

'Okay. I'll come.' She gave him a small, tight smile as he reached out, his hand drawing her to him. 'But I'm warning you: if you start with that pay grade stuff again I might just push you out of the helicopter.'

Aside from the noise of the rotor blades, inside the helicopter cabin it was quiet—sombre, almost. Watching the lights of Miami grow closer, Addie was aware of nothing but Malachi's still, silent presence beside her.

It was clear that his parents were alive and well, and she wondered what was serious enough to drag him over to the mainland. But, sticking to her word, she hadn't asked him any more about the phone call and he hadn't told her anything. However, he *had* held her hand during the entire three-hour flight.

After the peace of the island, downtown Miami felt crowded and noisy. But at least it was crowded with ordinary people, she thought nervously, staring out of the window as the limousine slid to a stop in front of the Marlin—one of Miami's swankiest and most exclusive Art Deco hotels. Malachi's parents were any-

thing *but* ordinary. Having furtively searched for them
on the internet, while he was talking to the pilot, she
had been horrified to discover that Henry and Serena
King were not only fabulously wealthy, glamorous and
beautiful, they also hosted some of the most decadent
parties around the globe.

Glancing at her reflection in the window, she felt
a rush of panic. Her dress was short, black and cute,
and it showed off her long legs, but it most certainly
wasn't decadent. Maybe she should have worn the dress
Malachi had given her instead. Her pulse shivered. Or
maybe she should have just stayed on the island.

'Are you okay?' Malachi glanced down at her, his
eyes roaming over her face.

'Yes. Why?'

He winced. 'Because you're cutting off the blood
supply to my hand.'

'Oh, sorry.' Loosening her grip, Addie felt her heart
start to thump loudly.

His eyes were dark and flickering with excitement,
and there was a strange almost nervous energy about
him that reminded her of how she had felt before playing in front of an audience: a mixture of fear and bravado and restlessness. But surely he didn't need to feel
like that. After all, they were his *parents*.

Glancing away, she looked up at the smooth, curving
hotel facade and frowned. 'I suppose I'm a little tense.
It feels like I've been away for ever,' she said carefully.

He studied her face in silence, and then slowly
pulled her up against him. 'Let me guess. You're worried about meeting Henry and Serena?'

She met his gaze. 'A little.'

'They're charming—and great company. I'm sure you'll fall under their spell. Everyone always does.'

He was smiling, but there was an undertone to his voice that she couldn't quite identify.

'I don't know if that's made me feel better or worse,' she said lightly. She squeezed his hand. 'Anyway, this isn't about me. It's about you—and I just want you to know that I meant what I said before. I'll be there for you.'

She glanced up at him, half expecting him to pull away or change the subject. But he didn't do either. Instead, after the briefest of hesitations, his fingers tightened around hers.

'I know.' His face softened and, lowering his mouth, he kissed her gently.

'Promise you'll stay close to me.'

She stared at him dazedly. 'I promise.'

It took nearly half an hour for them to make it up to the twelfth floor, where Malachi's parents were staying in the penthouse suite. Most of that was spent calming down the hotel manager, a tall, balding man who looked as though he was about to collapse but who eventually ended up offering them a magnum of champagne.

In the lift, watching the numbers counting up, Addie felt Malachi's gaze on her face.

'You look beautiful,' he said softly as with a slight shudder the lift came to a stop.

And then the doors opened and she caught her breath. Whatever she had been expecting, it wasn't this. The suite was huge, with high soaring ceilings. Six massive chandeliers swayed gently above a marble tiered fountain. But it wasn't the decor that had made her breath stop in her throat.

It was the people. Despite the room's size, it was packed. Women dressed in sequins and lace and men in dark suits were lounging on sofas or leaning against the walls; others were sprawled over chairs or one another. But all of them were wearing masks. *Masks!*

She glanced up nervously at Malachi but he was already leading her by the hand, weaving through the laughing, dancing crowd to the other side of the room to a table where two huge gold bowls sat side by side, each one filled with a selection of masks.

'I don't know which one to choose,' Addie said slowly. For some reason she couldn't bring herself to touch them.

'Then don't.'

His eyes were glittering and she could feel his body pulsing with that same nervous energy she had felt in the car, but his voice was surprisingly gentle.

'We don't have anything to hide.'

As they pushed their way through the mass of people, Malachi reached out and grabbed two glasses from a passing waiter. Holding the glasses up to the fountain, he let them fill with the bubbling liquid.

Tentatively, Addie took a sip from hers. 'It's champagne!'

Malachi nodded and stared away, across the room, his face twisting. To a casual observer the party might seem to be in full flow, but given the ratio of alcohol

to people he knew it was just getting started. His skin
was crawling. What was he *doing* here? And why had
he brought Addie with him? Glancing over at her huge,
shell-shocked blue eyes, he felt his stomach tighten
painfully.

'Sometimes it's champagne and absinthe,' he said
flatly. 'Then things get really out of hand.'

Nodding, Addie glanced round the room, sipping her
drink nervously. 'Who *are* all these people?'

Malachi shrugged. 'Serena probably invited them.
She hates small parties and she likes new people. And
anything outrageous or forbidden.'

'And where are your parents?'

His face didn't alter but his eyes seemed suddenly
to glitter more brightly.

'They'll be in one of the private rooms, having a
party of their own.'

There was a crash behind her and a man wearing
some kind of feathered headdress toppled over, hands
flailing, his glass smashing to the floor.

Malachi reacted immediately. In one swift movement he had pulled her behind him and yanked the
man to his feet. 'Get some air,' he said coldly, giving
the man a little push, and then turning back to Addie,
he said quietly, 'Come on. Let's go find Henry and
Serena.'

They found them easily enough. At the end of a cor-
ridor four huge men wearing dark suits stood barring
a door marked Private. And whatever was happening
behind them, it was a lot quieter and more civilised
than at the main party, Addie thought with relief. But as

the door opened she felt her heart lurch. The room was dimly lit, and there were far fewer people. But most of them appeared to be in a state of undress and some of them appeared to be…intimately joined.

She barely had time to take in what she was seeing when a beautiful blonde woman, wearing a shimmering dress that rippled over her body like molten silver, let out a scream and sashayed across the room towards them. Beside her, stumbling slightly, was a very handsome man with lipstick on his face and on his dress shirt. The woman gave a little wriggle, sending rainbows of light into the dark corners of the room, and kissed Malachi on both cheeks.

'Look, Henry! I'd said he'd come. I know you said we weren't to contact you, darling, but I don't deal with rude little men telling me what to do.'

'He's the hotel manager, Serena.' Malachi frowned. 'There's nearly two hundred people here. And the other guests are complaining.'

'How boring of them. And mean. Trying to spoil our fun.' Leaning forward, Serena ran her hand slowly over the lapel of Malachi's jacket. 'Not like *you*, darling. You can never resist a party, can you? And besides, you're so much better at managing those sort of people than Henry and I.'

Suddenly noticing Addie, she stopped.

'What exquisite hair! I had a red setter once, with fur that exact colour. It was my favourite dog. Mal, aren't you going to introduce us?'

Addie swallowed. *These were Malachi's parents.* Her heart began to pound. They were gorgeous. He had clearly inherited his high cheekbones from his mother and from his father his dark hair and those gleaming grey eyes.

'This is Addie.' She felt his hand on her back. 'Addie Farrell. Addie—this is Henry and Serena King.'

'What a sweet name,' Serena purred, and then, clapping her hands excitedly, she waved at one of the waiters. 'Four Brandy Alexanders. Make them doubles!'

Sipping her cocktail, Addie tried to look as though she was enjoying herself. Inside, though, she was in shock. All around her she was aware of the other guests, of bodies merging and soft moans, and of Malachi's taut profile and his hand gripping hers so tightly that she could feel her fingers going numb.

There was no love or tenderness in this room, just greed and narcissism and lust, and her heart contracted as she tried to imagine what it must have been like to grow up surrounded by these people. If this was his version of intimacy, it was no wonder he struggled so much to understand hers.

Watching Addie's hand tighten around her glass, Malachi tried to relax. He barely registered the other guests, or what they were doing; he'd seen it too many times before. Usually at his parents' parties he could find a place inside himself, somewhere to retreat. But with Addie beside him he had no choice but to stay focused, and it was as if he was seeing it all through her eyes—every sordid detail magnified and spotlit—and it sickened him.

As his gaze shifted from Addie's face to her tight fists, he felt her disgust too. Rage clawed at his stomach and reluctantly he let go of her hand. 'I've just got to talk to Serena and Henry for a minute,' he said slowly.

'Do you want me to come too?'

Meeting her gaze, he shook his head. 'I'll be right back. Just wait here.'

He turned to where his parents were draped over one another on a chaise longue, their eyes glittering like dark stars.

His mother smiled up at him mockingly. 'Malachi! Henry and I were just talking about you.'

Taking hold of his hand, Serena pulled him down onto the cushions beside her as his father stood up unsteadily.

'Darling,' she murmured. 'We *love* your little red-head.'

'Her name's Addie,' he said slowly.

'And it was so *clever* of you to find her. Henry is absolutely smitten.' Slowly, Serena ran her finger along his jawline. 'And you do look so like your father, don't you…?'

Malachi felt his skin grow taut; his pulse was pounding in his ears.

'She's with *me*, Serena.'

'Of course she is.' Her face hardened. 'It's just a bit of fun.'

He stared at her in shock. 'It's not fun. It's sick.'

His mother shook her head. 'Oh, dear. Somebody's having a tantrum.' She smiled at him coldly. 'And after all we've done for you.' She shrugged, her fingers curling under his chin. 'How very dull you are. Well, don't expect me to do your dirty work. You can tell Henry yourself.' Her eyes narrowed. 'If it's not too late.'

Glancing past her, Malachi felt his heart jolt. Across the room, his father was smiling at Addie, his face soft but his eyes dark and predatory. With the blood suddenly buzzing inside his head like a swarm of angry bees, Malachi pushed his mother's hand away from his face, stood up and crossed the room.

'Serena always likes the drinks too strong,' he heard his father say confidingly. 'Why don't you come with me? I can find you something soft to drink. Or maybe you'd like to lie down for a bit—'

He broke off abruptly, his mouth hanging open in fear as Malachi stepped in front of him, his face blazing with white-hot anger.

'The only one lying down will be you, Henry. In a hospital bed!' His voice was like ice. 'What the hell are you doing?'

Malachi drew a jagged breath. His body felt as if it was in free fall. Addie was staring at him, transfixed, but he couldn't bring himself to meet her gaze. Instead, grabbing her hand, he pulled her behind him protectively and turned towards his father.

'You couldn't help yourself, could you?' He shook his head, anger vying with pain, choking him, blistering his throat and mouth. 'Only you've gone too far. This isn't some stupid game. It's twisted.' Breathing out unsteadily, he took a step backwards. 'We're leaving. You have until three o'clock tomorrow to get out. But don't expect me to pick up the tab. This one's on you.'

Turning, he pulled Addie close, his heart jerking
with relief as his arm curled around her soft body.

'And don't bother trying to contact me. There won't
be any point. As of this moment, I never want to hear
from you again.'

Later, Addie would wonder how they made it to the airport. She had no memory of leaving the hotel or getting
in the limo or onto the plane. Nothing had seemed to
register on her brain except Malachi's rage. She didn't
think she had ever seen anyone so angry. His fury had
been like the burning cold of an ice storm.

Gazing across the plane's lounge, to where he sat
alone, she felt her stomach cramp. She didn't really
understand all that had happened at the party. All she
knew was that since getting in the limo she hadn't been
able to reach him. That he hadn't needed her and certainly hadn't wanted her.

Slumped on a sofa, gripping a pack of cards in his
hand, Malachi felt a wave of exhaustion wash over
him. He had gone to the hotel to stop the police getting involved and he should have left after seeing the
manager. Only he hadn't. He'd heard the music and the
laughter and he'd been like a hunting dog following a
scent. Only seeing Addie in the centre of that debauchery he'd immediately realised his mistake. Her shock,
her horror, had been like a slap to the face. Yes, those
guests had been happy to be there, and it had all been
consensual, but it was so messed up. And then Henry
had tried—

He gritted his teeth.

How could his father have done that? It had been obvious that Addie was with him. He shouldn't have even had to tell them that she was off limits. And then, of course, when he had, it had only spurred them on.

But he didn't care about them. Remembering Addie's face when his father had held out his hand, he felt sick. What if he hadn't been there? Anything could have happened. Imagining her fear, her confusion, he felt his chest tighten with a pure, savage rage.

Addie stood up. She felt tired—more than tired. She felt bruised by everything that had happened and too drained to fight for what Malachi clearly didn't even want to discuss. But she wasn't about to leave him alone. Slowly, she walked across the cabin.

'Where are you going?'

His words stopped her in her tracks. Hearing the strain in his voice, she stared at him uncertainly. 'I was going to get some water.' She hesitated. 'Would you like some? Or I could get you something stronger.'

'Something stronger.' His mouth twisted. 'So I can *drown my sorrows*?'

His voice was soft but she felt it slice through her like a knife.

'Maybe. Or we could talk—'

He shook his head. 'You think talking can change *this*.'

His face was pale, the skin stretched taut over his cheekbones as he laughed—only it didn't sound like a laugh. There was too much pain and anger there. And fear. But five weeks in a hospital bed had taught her to face fear; to resist anger, to overcome pain. And, lifting her chin, she nodded.

'Yes. I do. But you don't want to. You'd rather sit there and wallow—'

'You know *nothing* about my life,' he snarled.

Her pulse was pounding in her throat. Clenching her teeth, she glared at him. 'Yes, I do. I know you jumped into a pool of sharks for a bet; I know you eat apples in the bath.' Her gaze shifted from his face to his hand. 'And I know you play cards when you feel tense or angry.'

He looked up at her silently and resentment surged through her. *He was impossible and this was hopeless.*

She turned to walk away.

'Addie.'

Looking down, she saw he was touching her wrist, his fingers trembling against her skin.

'Don't go. Please.'

She stood, staring past him. 'Why should I stay?'

He breathed out unsteadily. 'You said you'd be there for me.'

She didn't reply at first and then finally, after what felt like the longest moment, she sighed and sat down on the sofa.

He held out the deck of cards, his face strained, uncertain. 'What would you like to play?'

She shook her head. 'I'm not sure I can. My brain doesn't seem to be working.'

Nodding slowly, he half smiled. 'My parents have that effect on people.'

He let out a long, slow breath and his smile faded. She waited.

Finally, hesitantly, he reached out and took her hand, his face filled with angry bewilderment. 'I find it hard.'

The words sounded as if they were being dragged from him.

Her chest squeezed tight. 'What do you find hard?'

'Choosing not to be like them.' He ran a hand wearily over his face. 'For years I had no choice. Even when I was little they'd drag me to parties and nightclubs.' He paused and gave her another taut smile. 'They didn't see why having me around should stop them doing what they wanted. And if I was difficult, then they'd just leave me behind.'

'Where?' Addie felt her heart thump painfully hard.

He shrugged. 'With their friends. And by "friends" I mean the people who found it hardest to say no to them.' Glancing up, he caught sight of her face and his mouth twisted. 'I don't know what was worse. Worrying that they would never come back or knowing they would.'

She stared at him, feeling his pain, the fear of a little boy abandoned by his so-called parents, his dread of their return. 'Why didn't they get a nanny?'

'They did. But they never stayed for more than a couple of weeks. It got better as I got older.' His eyes met hers. 'I got better at managing them.'

She swallowed. 'Is that why you went back to Miami?'

He looked away. 'Yes. They can charm their way

out of most situations. But sometimes, like last night, when they've gone too far and someone's threatening to call the police, I have to step in.' Smiling dully, he shrugged. 'It's irritating, but it's just easier and a lot less time-consuming if I sort it out.'

'And why did you leave? Tonight.'

She held her breath, sensing it was one question too many, but finally he turned to face her and the bleakness in his eyes almost broke her.

'I'd had enough,' he said quietly. 'Of their games. With them, it's always a game. I just don't want to play any more.'

He fell silent.

Not trusting herself to speak, Addie sat mute beside him. How could anyone survive that kind of damage? It was almost worse than what had happened to her. That had been an accident. This had been deliberate, sustained. But the outcome was the same: a shattered life, a damaged soul. And she knew exactly what it took to repair that damage. It needed acceptance and hope and patience.

And love.

Her eyes suddenly filled with tears and she closed them quickly, trying to stop them from falling, trying to block out the truth. Except she couldn't. The truth was that she loved him—still, and so much.

And it was time for her to accept that fact.

She opened her eyes and concentrated on her breathing. But it was not the time to share it. Now she needed to keep her promise. To be there for Malachi. Without thinking, she reached forward and slid her arms around him. After a moment's hesitation his arms tightened around her. They held each other in silence, their hearts beating in time together, until finally Addie shifted free.

'Come on. Let's go to bed.'

Standing up, he glanced out of the plane's window and frowned. A pale yellow line was already edging the dark sky. 'I'm sorry, sweetheart, I don't think we're going to get much sleep. We'll be landing in less than an hour.'

She smiled. 'Who said anything about sleep?'

His eyes locked on to hers and for a moment, she stared at him, hypnotised by their fierce dark longing. And then he reached down and, scooping her into his arms, he began to carry her towards the staircase.

CHAPTER NINE

IT WAS LATE afternoon in Caracas. Staring out over the city from the balcony of Malachi's suite, Addie let the straps of her camisole slip down over her shoulders to catch some sun.

Two hands slid around her waist. 'Afternoon, sleepy-head.'

Her heart started to pound as Malachi kissed her shoulder, his lips drifting languidly down over her throat.

'You were sleeping so deeply I thought I was going to have to wake you with a kiss,' he murmured.

The hands round her waist were beginning to drift too, slipping under the silk camisole, circling and caressing the bare skin of her belly, then reaching up to stroke her breasts, caressing her nipples until she was shaking with desire.

Unable to stop herself, she moaned softly and she felt his body stiffen, his fingers stilling.

'You did that earlier,' she said hoarsely. 'That's why I was so tired.'

His hands were moving again, sliding slowly over skin.

'In that case I think you should lie down right now,' he said, and, gently he dragged her back into the suite and onto the huge bed.

Later, feeling warm and dazed, she lay beside him, watching him devour the brunch that had been delivered. As he pushed the last forkful of eggs Benedict into his mouth, she gave him a mischievous smile and started clapping.

Draining his coffee cup, he grinned, eyes gleaming. 'I was hungry. And you want me to keep my strength up, don't you?'

Remembering their feverish lovemaking, she felt a melting heat ripple out from somewhere deep inside. *Yes, she did.* Only 'want' seemed too feeble a word to describe how fiercely she craved him.

'I'll try to be less demanding tonight,' she said lightly. 'Shouldn't you be getting ready?'

Rolling onto her side, she watched him get dressed. His pale grey shirt was still unbuttoned to the waist and she stared hungrily at the smooth, flat muscles of his stomach. Even half dressed, and with his hair still damp from the shower, there was a glamour to him that set him apart from other people, turned heads. It wasn't just his looks. It was something to do with that air of detachment, of being alone in a crowd.

Thinking back to his parents' party, she felt a rush of protectiveness. It was no wonder he had chosen to stay alone, or that he found it so difficult to let people get close to him. But he was changing. Look at how he had opened up to her last night. It might not have been his whole life story, but it had been a brief glimpse into what had made him the man he was. And it was the first time he had ever even hinted that he might need her. And surely with need came love?

She glanced up, her heart aching. She longed to tell him that she loved him but she knew it was too soon. She had barely come to terms with how she felt. If she sprung her feelings on Malachi it would be disastrous. Like trying to put a head collar on a wild mustang. She needed to follow her own advice and be patient. But there was nothing to stop her from showing she cared.

Trying to keep her face as casual as possible, she sat up, pulling the sheet over her breasts. 'How are you feeling?'

Stepping away from the wardrobe, he turned to face her, frowning. 'Fine. A little tired.' The corners of his mouth curled upwards.

She smiled back at him, then hesitated. 'I actually meant how are you feeling about last night?'

He was still smiling, but the smile was set and still. After a moment he shrugged. 'That's fine too.'

Turning away, he reached into the wardrobe and she stared at his back uncertainly. Was that it? Last night he had seemed so desperate, so tormented. But it was clear that as far as he was concerned the conversation was over.

'Which one?' He held out two ties for inspection. 'Or do you not like either of them?'

Pushing aside her thoughts, she looked up at him and frowned. 'What's it for again?'

He held her gaze. 'It's a meeting with the mayor and the council members.'

'The blue one, then.'

'I like the red one.'

'Then wear the red one.' Stretching out her legs on top of the sheet, she smiled up at him innocently, her eyes dancing. 'If you don't mind looking like a gigolo.'

He raised an eyebrow. 'A gigolo?'

She bit her lip. 'Maybe you could wear some of those nice stacked shoes we saw in that shop.

His eyes had narrowed and he was moving slowly towards the bed like a predatory animal. 'Anything else?'

'A manbag?' She gave a shriek of laughter as he grabbed hold of her leg and pulled her down the bed towards him, pinning her arms above her head.

'A manbag…' he repeated slowly, his eyes roving over her naked body. 'I'm not sure if I really see myself with one of those. But you might be right about the tie. In fact, I think you might look better wearing it.'

Too late, she read the intent in his eyes. 'No, Malachi—you can't!'

'Oh, but I can,' he said softly, and the heat in his gaze would have stripped the clothes from her skin if she hadn't already been naked.

With deliberate slowness he twisted the tie around her wrists and pulled it over the elaborate gilded bedstead, knotting it with one practised hand. Twisting, Addie tried to pull her hands free, but she simply managed to tighten her bonds.

'There,' he said softly, letting go of her wrists. 'I knew it would look better on you.'

He stared down at her, eyes dark with passion and

unwavering, and she felt a hot ache spread out over her skin.

'You can't leave me tied up here, Malachi,' she said quickly, trying to push aside the thought that in all probability he could. 'What about when the maids come to clean the suite?'

He smiled, a long, slow smile. 'I'll tell them to leave it until tomorrow.'

'Malachi! Untie me.'

'What will you give me if I do?'

'You need to worry about what I'll give if you don't! Now, untie me!' She stared up at him, torn between wanting to laugh and wanting to give him a black eye.

He grinned. 'Is that right? I'm not sure you're in any position to be issuing threats here, sweetheart.' He sighed. 'However, fortunately for you, life has taught me that there is one absolute unbreakable rule when it comes to staying in hotels.'

He tugged at the knot and she slipped her wrists free.

'And that is, don't do anything to upset the house-keeping staff.'

She punched him gently. 'So letting me go has nothing to do with my persuasive charms, then?'

His eyes were still tinged with passion, but softer now. 'Believe me, you're *very* persuasive, sweetheart, but—' Grimacing, he sat up and twitched the sheet over her naked body. 'I have *got* to go to this meeting.' Seeing her expression, he shook his head. 'Don't look at me like that. I'd love to get out of this but I can't.'

His hand moved over the sheet, following the contours of her breasts and belly, and she felt her skin grow warm and tingling.

'You can find out what that feels like later.' Eyes glittering, he stood up. 'I'll even let you choose the tie.'

After he'd left, Addie spent a relaxing two hours in the hotel spa, having a facial and full-body massage. Malachi had left a message telling her that he had arranged for Lupita, a personal stylist, to come to their suite, and she arrived promptly, with several rails of beautiful clothes, an array of shoes and a box of jewellery that came with an armed bodyguard.

It was exhausting, but enormous fun. Lupita not only seemed to have met everyone who was anyone in Caracas, she was also talented at her job, knowing exactly which outfits would make Addie look and feel good.

Finally having made her choice, all that remained was to get ready.

Smoothing foundation over her skin, she stared at her reflection critically.

It was lucky that people could only see what was on the outside. And she was a lot less nervous about meeting Malachi's guests than she had been about finally coming face-to-face with his parents.

She applied mascara, blinked and reapplied it.

But being nervous had some advantages. At least it meant she could hardly think straight. Certainly not about what everyone would be saying about her tonight. It had been different at the masked party. Everyone there had been hiding who they were. But tonight there would be reporters and photographers, and Malachi would be looking to generate as much publicity as possible for the opening of his first casino in South America.

Her heart gave a jolt of hope. But what did that mean for her? She knew what she wanted it to mean. She wanted to forget the past—forget this stupid deal and be his wife again.

But it was so much more complicated than that.

Thankfully her hairdresser chose that moment to arrive, and she was able to push aside her troubling thoughts.

An hour later Addie breathed out in relief as the young woman styling her hair stepped back and smiled.

'You look very beautiful, Ms Farrell.'

Turning her head from side to side, Addie stared into the mirror with pleasure. She had decided, on Lupita's advice, to put her hair up in a French pleat. It was not something she had ever done before, preferring the simplicity of a ponytail for work or a low chignon for more dressy occasions. But now she was glad she had followed the stylist's advice.

'Thank you!' She smiled up at the hairdresser.

The girl looked pleased. 'I think Mr King will be very happy,' she said shyly.

Addie took another quick glance at herself. Hopefully he would. She would soon find out.

Staring round the casino floor, Malachi felt a rush of satisfaction. The building had been derelict when he'd first seen it. Originally an opera house, it had been abandoned after a fire had damaged most of the stage, and then it had simply been left to decay. Only he had seen its potential. Not as an opera house. The capital city of Venezuela already had one of those. But as a casino.

It had taken six months just to clear the site and make it safe to work in. Another year to rebuild the interior and bring it up to modern health and safety standards. Then another five months painstakingly recreating the original gilded domed ceiling and setting up the casino floor.

His vision had been clear. No cool, contemporary chic. He had wanted old-style glamour. Gilt and glass and glitter. And it had been worth it, he thought triumphantly. It looked incredible: a gilded, show-stopping interior that mixed fin-de-siècle opulence with an unmistakable whiff of the forbidden and decadent.

And yet there was something that didn't feel quite right. Some detail he had overlooked. Something was missing, but he couldn't quite put his finger on it...

The next moment his uncertainty was forgotten as yet another swathe of local VIPs stepped forward to offer their congratulations. Twenty minutes later, though, he was staring round the room again, the famous King smile in place, while his brain clicked through the evening's schedule, looking for glitches.

Only there was nothing out of place. Frowning, he glanced up at one of the boxes he'd insisted be kept during the refurbishment, and caught a flash of red hair, a glimpse of long leg and felt his chest tighten.

Addie! She was here.

He was shocked by how happy that made him feel— happy then stunned as he realised that *she* had been what was missing. Abruptly his elation faded as the woman turned and waved excitedly at a friend in the crowd. It was not Addie. And her hair wasn't even red. He must have been hallucinating! Seeing what he wanted to see.

His words echoed inside his head and he felt a momentary flicker of unease. Did he really want to see *her* that badly?

Eyes narrowing, he gazed across the room. There were so many beautiful women here tonight. Why was he obsessing over Addie when he could just pluck one of them out from the crowd?

Because he didn't want just any woman. He wanted Addie.

His heart began to thump. But it was inevitable really, he reassured himself. He'd been spending so much time with her that he'd got used to having her around. And with her glorious red hair and beautiful curving body she was there for a very specific reason. To stand out—to be seen by his side. Together they would be the most dazzling, the most desired couple in the room.

He frowned. But where the hell *was* she?

And then he saw her.

And this time there could be no mistake.

She was standing at the top of the wide, curving staircase that led down to the main casino floor, the two bodyguards he had assigned to protect her on either side of her.

Caught beneath a pool of light, she looked beautiful. More than beautiful, he thought dazedly. She looked like a goddess. Her heels were black and high but her dress was dark red and short, with long sleeves. It clung to her curves as though she had been sewn into it.

But as she stared down into the crowded casino he felt her hesitation, saw the uncertainty in her eyes. He was moving even before he realised he was doing so—striding across the room and up the stairs.

She saw him just as he reached her side, her ruby and diamond earrings catching the light as she turned to greet him.

He stared at her, his heart in his throat. Up close, she looked even more stunning. Her long hair was swept up, revealing her slim neck and flawless face, and suddenly he couldn't stand it any more. He had to touch her. More than touch—he wanted to lay claim to her.

Reaching out, he took her hand and drew her slowly towards him. 'You look beautiful, sweetheart. I think you should keep these.' Gently he touched her earrings. 'And that dress looks divine on you.'

She smiled then, her uncertainty fading, and it was as though they were alone; around them the swarming mass of people melted away.

'Thank you. I wasn't sure about the length. But I think covering my arms balances out my legs.'

He nodded. He had no idea what she was talking about. Just looking at her was throwing him off balance. 'I agree. Or I would if I knew what you meant.'

She pinched his hand. 'There are *rules*, you know. About clothing.'

His eyes gleamed. 'Has this got something to do with the tie—?'

'Malachi!' She glanced nervously over her shoulder, her body twisting, and suddenly he was too jolted to breathe, let alone speak.

Cut low and draped at the back, whatever rules she had been talking about, that dress was breaking all of them. His eyes bumped down the curve of her spine, his blood thickening and slowing, his thoughts a heaving mass of yearning, unfocused desire.

Trying to bring order back to the chaotic disarray of his body and mind, he dragged his eyes away from the smooth, golden temptation of her bare skin and gestured at a passing waiter.

'Here!' Back in control once more, he handed her a fluted glass of champagne. 'Let's go and mingle. There are some people I want you to meet.'

The rest of the evening was a blur of people and names. Addie felt as if she was floating. Beside her, one of the bodyguards held up a protective arm as guests spilled past them and she glanced up at him dazedly.

Bodyguard! When had she become the sort of person who needed a bodyguard?

The thought made her head spin. But then it was spinning anyway. She was so nervous she had barely even registered the gorgeous over-the-top decor—in fact, she'd been aware of very little except the sidelong glances that had followed her and Malachi as they made their way around the room, his hand resting casually on her back.

'They're all looking at us,' she'd whispered as he'd led her through the crowd.

'They're not,' he had whispered back. 'They're looking at you.'

But of course they hadn't been.

It was Malachi who was the object of their curious and admiring attention. He was the reason the hum of conversation tailed off. The reason men stood taller, waiters moved with even more swift efficiency and women—

She breathed in sharply. *All* the women were in his fan club, if the furtive, hungry expressions on their faces were anything to go by.

But of course they were. He was devastatingly handsome—and in a dinner jacket at his most desirable, with the stark contrast of black and white emphasising his flawless bone structure and restless grey eyes. Moreover, it was his night—his name on a thousand lips.

And she was the woman holding his arm. His wife.

Except that at no point had Malachi made that clear to anyone. Her heart began to pound. *Just who was she supposed to be tonight?* And was everyone else thinking the same thing?

Malachi stared across the casino floor, struggling to adjust his thoughts. Normally on an evening like this he would have been acting on autopilot: smiling, chatting, working the room. But tonight he just couldn't seem to concentrate. Not with Addie so close to him, the bare skin of her back so soft and tempting. If only he could peel off that dress and see the rest of her—

She was so beautiful, so desirable. Every woman in

the room wanted to be her and every man wanted her.
But she was his wife.

His wife.

So why not tell the world?

He glanced around the room. Everywhere he looked
there were couples. Men and women holding hands,
looking up at one another in excitement, sharing their
happiness. His chest felt tight; his mouth was suddenly
dry. He wanted to touch Addie and hold her close. But
deep down he knew that they had no future. No sex,
however perfect, was enough to make a marriage happy
or healthy. He knew that better than anyone.

They were standing beside the roulette table. Beside him, the casino manager, Edgar, was talking to
the young male croupier.

Malachi nodded at them. 'Are we busy?'

The croupier nodded. 'Yes, sir. Very busy. Roulette
is very popular with the ladies.'

Malachi grinned. 'It always is.'

Beside him, Edgar cleared his throat. 'Would you
like to play, Mr King? Or maybe...' Glancing past Malachi, the manager smiled politely at Addie, hesitated.

Malachi stared at her profile in silence, feeling her
tension. He'd always known this moment would come:
the moment when he would have to formally introduce Addie and he knew that she was waiting for his
response. His chest felt tight. She was his wife, but he
didn't believe in happy-ever-after.

He met her gaze deliberately. 'Addie, this is Edgar
Baptista, my casino manager. Edgar, this is Miss Addie
Farrell.'

Addie stared at him in silence as slowly the meaning behind his words filtered through her nerves. *Miss Farrell.* Not *Mrs King.* Not *My wife.*

'They want you to spin the wheel.'

She gazed up at him through the confused tangle of misery and disappointment. 'Spin the what?'

He gestured towards the roulette wheel. 'It's a tradition. It brings good luck to the house.'

'I'm surprised you of all people believe in luck,' she said lightly, pushing down the hurt in her chest. 'You'll be telling me next you believe in the tooth fairy.'

His eyes met hers: dark, mocking, compelling.

'We have a saying in the casino, sweetheart. Luck is for losers. But it seems a little churlish to point that out right now.'

He smiled at her then—one of those devastating smiles that made her heart beat too fast.

'Besides, everyone needs a bit of luck in their lives, don't you think? For when the odds are really against them.'

Only of course the odds never were against Malachi. How could they be? He was the man who set them.

Finally the evening was over. As they left the casino photographers crowded onto the steps, calling out to Malachi, cameras flashing on every side as he replied with his usual sangfroid.

'What do they want?' she whispered.

'They want to know who you are.' His eyes were cool.

'What did you tell them?' She swallowed, trying to hide her longing.

'I told them I wasn't going to do their job for them.'

It was a good answer. Plausible and playful. And evasive. A perfect bluff, in fact.

Her heart was hammering so loudly it took her a moment to realise that the press were still shouting at them.

'What are they saying now?' she said dully as he slid his arm around her waist.

'They want a photo.' He smiled down at her.

'Haven't they got enough?'

'They want a very particular kind of photo,' he said softly and, pulling her firmly against him, he lowered his head and kissed her.

Light exploded around them, and despite herself Addie felt her stomach curl as he deepened the kiss to the roar of the photographers. It was over in a moment.

Lifting his head, he smiled at her lazily. 'There. Now everyone's happy!'

Except she wasn't. Instead she felt restless, on edge—like a warrior getting ready for battle.

To Addie, the suite felt strangely still and quiet after the noise and drama of the casino.

Pulling loose his tie, Malachi walked slowly round her, studying her appraisingly, stopping behind her. Then, moving forward, he slowly began to stroke the back of her neck. 'So. Did you enjoy yourself tonight?'

Addie nodded. She couldn't run away from what had happened at the casino, but already her skin was tingling, her body leaning into his. 'It was fun. I'm just sad it's all over—'

Her pulse jerked as she felt his lips brush against

her throat, and suddenly she was desperate for him to kiss her properly.

'Don't worry,' he murmured, tipping her head back, his mouth teasing hers. 'The fun's only just beginning...'

Staring up at the moonlight, Malachi walked slowly across the rooftop terrace and sat down on a concrete bench. His face was impassive but his head was in turmoil. It had been a perfect evening. The casino had run like clockwork. All the VIPs had gone home happy. Everything had gone according to plan.

And Addie—she had played her part to perfection. She had been the most beautiful woman in the room. In that dark red dress she had been more intoxicating than a bottle of claret. All eyes had followed her around the room and having her beside him, her arm curled through his, had felt *right*. It had felt *good*.

His mouth twisted. Only that was the problem. He didn't want it to feel good or right. Any more than he'd wanted to feel so out of control when he'd seen her with his father.

The truth was he didn't want to feel anything at all.

A muscle tightenend in his jaw. He'd rather jump into a pool of sharks. It would certainly be less dangerous. Less painful. Although he knew he was probably alone in thinking that way.

His stomach tightened. But that was the point. He *was* alone. He always had been. And nothing and no one could change that fact. Especially not a woman who had traded sex for money.

'Malachi—'

He turned.

Addie stepped forward, her face hesitant beneath the moonlight. 'Is everything okay?'

He nodded. 'Of course. I just needed some fresh air. Clear my head.' He frowned. 'You're dressed!'

She was wearing jeans and his dress shirt. Her face was flushed.

'I couldn't find you. I thought maybe you'd gone downstairs. Then I remembered about the roof garden, so I thought I'd check up here first.'

He smiled. 'I'm fine. I'm just a bit wired. It was a big night. Lots of things to get right.'

'You did a good job.' She smiled. 'It's a pity you can't give yourself some kind of reward.'

He took her waist in both hands and pulled her towards him. 'I did that earlier.'

She looked up at him, her eyes fixing on his face, her expression suddenly intent. 'Is that what I am? A reward?'

He stared past her, her words trapping him against the concrete, panic rising up inside. What the hell had he done? All those years he'd held it together, had never said a word about his parents or his childhood to anyone. Then Addie came back into his life, with her questions and her concern and her soft blue eyes, and all those barriers he'd built between the world and himself had come crashing down. And this was the consequence. This assumption that she had some right to cross-examine him, to expect answers.

But it was going to stop now.

'I like to think of you more as an asset.' He met her

gaze levelly. 'Which reminds me—I'm flying down to Rio tomorrow. To look at a casino. I thought maybe you'd like to come with me. It's a beautiful city. Perhaps we could go to Buenos Aires and Santiago. Maybe even Acapulco.'

Addie gazed at him warily, trying to contain the chaos and confusion inside. Something was happening. Something she didn't quite understand. He was inviting her to go away with him and yet his manner was strangely detached, careless almost.

It had been such a tough couple of days. His parents' party had been horrible. But for the first time she had actually understood what had made Malachi the man he was. And afterwards he had needed her—not for sex, but for comfort and support. They had seemed so close.

Only now that closeness felt like an illusion, a trick of her senses, for all evening he had deliberately chosen not to acknowledge her as his wife. And now he was inviting her to go to Rio with him. Not even as his mistress but as an *asset*—

Her heart bumped against her ribs as though it was warning her to stay quiet. But she couldn't run away from this conversation. Not this time. Not after everything that had happened. 'I'd love to go to all those places. But how does that fit in with our deal?'

There. She had said it. She watched his eyes narrow fractionally.

Malachi stared at her in silence.

Their deal! A thread of anger and frustration uncoiled like a snake in the pit of his stomach. He could see the tension in her face, the doubt and unease, and he knew what she wanted him to say. But he would never say it. He couldn't.

His chest grew tight. He felt hard, cruel, knowing how much he was about to hurt her. But he couldn't give her what she needed.

Meeting her gaze, he smiled at her coolly. 'I'm not sure I understand the question, sweetheart. Nothing's changed except our location.'

He watched her eyes widen.

'I don't care about the location—' she began.

'So it's about the money?' he said smoothly.

It was as though he had slapped her.

'The money? No, it's not about the money!' she protested.

Her face was flushed and he could see a pulse beating at the base of her throat.

'It's about us.'

'"Us"?' he repeated softly.

'Yes. *Us.* You and me. Doing a tour of South America. How does that work, Malachi?'

She stared at him defiantly, but he heard the catch in her voice.

'I'm saying let's go to Rio. And then we'll take it from there. One day at a time.'

Her face shifted, softened. 'So you want to try again? Properly, I mean?'

He felt his chest clench painfully at the question. The hope in her eyes took his breath away. For a moment it made him hope and believe that it could work.

That maybe he could need her and love her and care about her as she cared about him.

And then, slowly his hope faded, his eyes slid past her to the spiral staircase leading back down to their suite *and to escape*. It was no good. He might have let Addie get close, closer than anyone ever had, but he couldn't handle it. Couldn't handle caring or needing or loving. He'd tried for so many years with his parents and look where *that* had got him.

But she didn't need to share his fear and pain and guilt and anger. Slowly, deliberately, he met her gaze. 'I don't remember saying that.'

Addie looked at him in confusion. 'You said we'd take things one day at a time. You just said it.'

'I meant carry on as we are one day at a time. Or a week at a time, if you prefer. Obviously there won't be the same financial terms, but I'm happy to give you an allowance.'

She felt dizzy; her breathing was all wrong—jerky and out of time. For a moment she felt flattened. Earlier, standing by his side in that beautiful gilded room, she had actually started to believe in them…in their future. But now she realised that whatever future they might have had it had ended before it had ever begun.

'A week at a time…?' she echoed. Her heart seemed to be shrinking, its beat slowing. Was he actually offering to keep her on as his mistress on a weekly basis?

'If you prefer.' He shrugged. 'We can see how it goes.'

She nodded mechanically, unable to speak. And then, glancing down, she realised he was still holding her by the waist. Breathing in, she reached down and pushed his hands away.

'You utter bastard,' she said slowly. 'What is *wrong* with you? How can you sit there and suggest this? That I be your mistress on some kind of zero-hours contract like I'm a chambermaid?' She shook her head; her stomach was churning.

His eyes were cold. 'You're being irrational. I'm simply offering the same deal with slightly modified terms. If it's the money that's a problem—'

'Go to hell!' she snarled. Her hands curling into fists, she took a step backwards. 'I can't believe this,' she whispered. 'I actually thought we could try again. That we could give our marriage a second chance. I must have been out of my mind.'

'If you thought I was going to renew my vows to a woman who slept with me for money, then I'd have to agree with you,' he said coldly.

Stepping forward, she slapped him across the face.

For a moment there was no sound except the distant downtown traffic and her frantic, uneven breathing.

Her eyes were wide and stunned, as though he had slapped *her.* 'I can't do this any more. I know loving you is hard. I did it before and it nearly broke me. I wanted to keep fighting for us. But I can't. I've got to think of myself now, and you will never give me what I need—how can you? You don't have it to give, Malachi.'

He took a step towards her, his eyes fixed on her face. 'You need to calm down.'

She stared at him, her whole body trembling. 'No. I need to leave.'

Turning, she began to walk, then run towards the staircase.

'We have a deal, Addie.' His voice was like ice.

Her foot was on the top step as she turned to face him. 'So sue me. And while you're at it you can divorce me too.'

And, grabbing hold of the rail, she ran lightly down the stairs.

CHAPTER TEN

STORMING BACK INTO the suite, Addie stared wildly around the elegant room, blind to its beauty. Tears of anger and disbelief were burning her throat and she barely knew what she was doing. All her efforts, every thought, every breath, were concentrated on one goal. Getting as far away as possible from the man who had broken her heart for the second time.

Even though it meant she would never see him again.

A wave of misery hit her head-on and she had to press her hand over her mouth to stop herself from crying out loud. For one mad moment she thought about running back upstairs to tell him she'd changed her mind.

But if she stayed, if she accepted his offer, what did she think was going to happen?

Surely she didn't actually believe that Malachi was going to wake up one morning and miraculously be in love with her? If love meant honesty and trust and sharing more than just bodies then he didn't know *how* to love. Seeing him with his parents, feeling his pain and confusion after their party, had felt like a defining moment in their relationship. As if from then on things would be different between them. Only it could never be any different. She saw that now—saw that he was way too damaged, too detached, ever to love her as she needed to be loved.

His insulting offer to renew their 'deal' had simply made that fact undeniable.

She let out a long, slow breath. Facing the facts, while not pleasant, at least made her options clear. She had made a mistake—a stupid, humiliating mistake—by agreeing to his stupid, humiliating deal. But at least she had only traded sex for money. To stay would be a far bigger mistake, for she would be trading her self-respect for a bunch of worthless dreams.

She wasn't going to give her heart to a man who thought a woman's role was to look beautiful and glamorous and provide sex. Nor was she going to shed any more tears.

Catching sight of her handbag, she snatched it up gratefully. It had everything she needed: money, and most important, her passport. She wanted nothing else—not even her own clothes; all of them were unwearable now anyway—sullied by that horrible, insulting offer he'd made to her.

Stepping into the waiting lift, she squared her shoulders. But as the lift slid slowly to a stop she felt some of her bravado fade. Now what? She couldn't just sit around in the reception area. But the hotel was nowhere near the airport. And although she might have braved public transport during daylight, she didn't feel confident about tackling the metro on her own in the early hours of the morning.

There was no avoiding it. She was going to have to speak to someone at the main desk about ordering a taxi. She certainly wasn't going to get to the airport otherwise. Her chest tightened. But there was no other way.

She walked quickly across the foyer. Behind the desk, the young receptionist looked up from her computer screen and smiled, and said in near perfect English, 'Good morning. My name is Carolina. How may I help you?'

Addie was about to reply when the girl's smile faded, a blush colouring her cheeks and brow. 'I'm so sorry. It's Ms Farrell, isn't it? You're staying in the Cruz-Rojas suite with Mr King.'

Nodding, Addie gripped the edge of the desk and forced herself to smile.

'Yes. That's right.' Horrified that the girl might be about to start asking questions about her stay, she said quickly, 'I wonder, would it be possible for you to order a taxi for me? To take me to the airport?'

Her lungs seemed to shrivel inside her chest as the girl shook her head apologetically. 'I'm sorry, Miss Farrell. We don't actually use taxis at this hotel. Most of our guests prefer their own transport.'

Addie felt her heart start to race. Of course they did. Like Malachi, they probably all had private cars with chauffeurs to take them wherever they wanted to go. She shivered. She would rather crawl over broken glass than go back upstairs to ask that monster for anything.

'But…' The receptionist looked at her earnestly. 'We *do* operate a complimentary limousine service to the airport. Would you like me to arrange one for you?'

'Oh, yes. Yes, please.' Addie felt a wave of gratitude wash over her. 'As soon as possible.'

She wasn't worried that Malachi would try and stop her. He hadn't even come after her when she'd stormed out of their wedding, and he hated scenes. But she felt so tired, and her self-control was slipping. She wasn't going to be able to hold it together for much longer—

'Miss Farrell?' It was the receptionist—Carolina. 'We have a limousine waiting for you outside. Your driver is Luis. Have a good trip.' She smiled shyly at Addie. 'Are you going somewhere nice?'

Addie nodded, emotion choking her.

Yes, she was. She was going home.

Everything was going to be all right. Soon Malachi King would be just a distant memory and she would marvel at the fact that he had ever had the power to hurt her.

Eyes narrowed, Malachi stared angrily across the empty roof garden. He couldn't believe what had just happened. What did she expect from him? In fact, why did she expect anything from him anyway?

His mouth curled in frustration. Throwing all those accusations at him and storming off like that. It was just like their wedding all over again.

And saying she wanted him to divorce her? The blood pounded in his ears. He had never even thought about a divorce. Probably he never would have if she hadn't thrown it in his face—

That thought was still uppermost in his mind when he felt his phone vibrate in his pocket. Skin tingling, half expecting it to be Addie, he pulled it out. Glancing at the screen, he felt his stomach tighten. It was a message from his father.

We're in New York, at the Aviation Club. Serena says to tell you we're having a party on Saturday. If you can behave, you're welcome to join us. Bring that sweet little redhead if you like. I attach a peace offering—

Malachi stopped reading. There was more—something to do with a money transfer—but he didn't care enough to finish the message. Opening up the attachment, he watched the bodies on the screen in silence. Abruptly, he switched it off.

He could almost hear Henry's cool, detached voice inside his head. *Bring that sweet little redhead if you like*. It knocked the breath out of his body that his father could actually suggest that. He had tried so hard to make it clear to Henry that Addie was out of bounds. So why—?

Lifting his head, he stared bleakly up at the moon, its pale, pure beauty making his heart contract. He knew why; he'd known why since he was a small child, only he had never wanted or been able to confront the truth before. But it was simple really.

For Henry and Serena drama and tension were more important than love and loyalty. For them life was a series of spectacles for which anything could be sacrificed—including their son's happiness. And when things—or people—got messy or boring, they simply got rid of them and moved on. The ground felt suddenly unsteady beneath his feet as he remembered what it had felt like: the unspoken threat, the fear that one day they would get rid of *him*.

Shakily he ran his hand over his face, panic swelling inside him. Only with shock he realised that he wasn't panicking about losing his parents.

But about losing Addie.

It hurt. Just thinking about her not being there.

Hurt because he loved her.

His heart gave a jerk as finally he faced the truth.

He loved her.

His face was impassive but his whole body was shaking. Why hadn't he realised?

He'd spent his entire life reading people. Spotting their weaknesses, their deceits and delusions. Yet he'd failed to notice that he was in love.

Worse, he had bullied and manipulated the woman he loved into being his mistress, using her loyalty to her charity to get his own way.

For a moment he stood frozen and then he turned.

He needed to explain, to apologise, to tell her how he felt. Now. Before it was too late.

Heart pounding, he started to walk, then run towards the staircase.

But where was she?

Downstairs, Malachi stared uneasily around the empty suite. He had imagined Addie to be hurtling around the room, tossing clothes into her suitcase. Only the bedroom felt still and lifeless. Slowly he checked the other rooms, his pulse racing. But she wasn't there.

She couldn't have actually left—

Feeling sick on the inside, he checked the rooms again. And then his heart jerked as he pulled open the wardrobe door. Her suitcase was still there—and all her clothes and shoes. He felt almost numb with relief. She would hardly abandon all her stuff if she was leaving him. At the very least she would take her handbag.

Glancing round, his heart missed a beat. It was gone and so was Addie. His breath felt suddenly tight and panicky in his chest and, crossing the room in three quick strides, he picked up the phone and rang Reception.

'Mr King. How may I help?'

'Miss Farrell—' he began.

'Yes, sir. The limousine has already left.'

He went cold.

'Left? When? Where?' The stunned silence at the end of the phone echoed inside his head. 'Where has she gone?' he demanded hoarsely, not caring that he sounded nothing like his cool public persona.

'To the airport. She left ten minutes ago.'

He barely heard the receptionist's trembling reply. Inside his head one question was repeating itself over and over again.

What have I done? What have I done? What have I done?

More importantly, what was he going to do now?

* * *

Gazing up out of the window of the limousine, Addie watched the lights of an aeroplane move slowly through the night sky, growing smaller and smaller until finally they disappeared altogether. She sighed. Soon she would be on a plane just like that one and all this—this misery and mess—would be left far behind. In another country. In another life.

She glanced slowly around the luxurious cream leather interior of the limousine. All this luxury would be gone soon too.

But she didn't care. None of it mattered. She would have traded all of it to make Malachi love her. To make her marriage work. Her heart squeezed inside her chest. She loved him so much. But it hadn't been enough.

Sighing, she glanced at the clock on the limousine's dashboard and then closed her eyes. If she was lucky she might be able to catch a flight back home in the next few hours, but it was going to be a long night and an even longer day tomorrow. Only she wasn't going to spend it wallowing in the past and in self-pity. She lifted her chin. From now on, she was only going to go forward.

After what felt like no time at all, the limousine slowed, and opening her eyes, she glanced out of the window as it slid to a stop. She frowned. What the hell was the chauffeur playing at? They weren't at the airport: they were back at the hotel.

Leaning forward she banged angrily on the screen behind his head. 'Excuse me…er…Luis? What are you doing? I want to go to the airport!'

Frantically she tried to think of the words in Spanish, but before she could even muster up a basic sentence he had got out of the car and opened her door.

'What is going on? *Hablo—habla inglès?*' she said, staring up at him in frustration. 'No. You don't understand. I need to go the *airport*—'

Still holding the door open, the chauffeur stared impassively ahead. Realising she was getting nowhere, Addie slid past him and stalked angrily back into the hotel and up to the reception desk.

'Hello,' she said breathlessly. 'It's Carolina, isn't it? I'm sorry, but your driver—I don't think he quite understands what I want him to do. He was supposed to be taking me to the airport but he's brought me back here.'

The girl bit her lip. 'I'm sorry, Miss Farrell. But he was given new instructions.'

Addie gazed at her in frustration. 'What do you mean, new instructions? I thought he was *my* driver.' She pointed in exasperation to where Luis stood, still looking straight ahead.

'He—he is,' the girl stammered. 'But there was a change of plan.'

Addie shook her head. 'Not by me. So who changed it?'

'That would be me!'

There was a long, frozen pause and then Addie turned slowly round. Standing in the centre of the foyer, Malachi was watching her, his eyes fixed on her face.

'Then I suggest you change it back again,' she

said through gritted teeth. Her heart was racing with anger.

Slowly he shook his head. 'That's not going to happen.'

'It's not up to you.' She stared at him furiously. 'You might be important to some people but you don't have any power in this hotel.'

He met her gaze. 'That's not strictly true. I *do* pay their wages.'

Her breath caught in her throat. 'Really?' she said coldly. 'By the day? Or by the week?'

A muscle flickered in his jaw. 'I think they're all quite happy with their contracts.'

'Lucky them,' she snapped. 'But, fascinating though this is, I'm sure you didn't drag me back here to discuss your staff's employment contracts. So what is it, Malachi? What do you want?'

'We didn't finish our conversation.'

'No, we did, Malachi. You just didn't have the last word.' She gave a tired laugh. 'Is that what this is about?' She shook her head, her mouth curving contemptuously. 'Fine, then—just say it. Go on.'

He glanced past her. 'Maybe we should take this somewhere a little more private.'

She felt the air punch out of her lungs. Shaking her head, she met his gaze. 'No. We should not. I'm not going anywhere with you, Malachi. So, short of abducting me, you're going to have say whatever it is you want to say right here.'

He stared at her in silence, his eyes never leaving her face. Finally he shrugged. 'As you wish.'

Glancing past her, he smiled.

'*Gracias, Carolina y Luis*. I can take it from here.'

Then before Addie had a chance to react, he had crossed the foyer and tipped her body up over his shoulders.

'Put me down!' Twisting, kicking, struggling, she beat her hands against his back. 'Malachi! You can't do this.' She felt his arm tighten around her legs and then, hearing the lift doors open, she began to yell. 'Call the police! I don't care if he's your boss—'

The lift doors closed in front of her.

'You can't do this! Put me down!'

Abruptly he leaned forward and she slid ignominiously from his shoulder. Immediately she rushed at him, but he caught her easily, holding her flailing arms by the wrists.

'Calm down. I'm not going to hurt you. I told you—I just want to talk.'

Yanking her arms away, she ignored him. Opening her bag, she pulled out her phone. 'I am going to call the police and have you arrested, and you can see how you like talking to them—'

Taking her phone away from her ear, she stared at the screen irritably.

'Let me guess. No signal?' Malachi said helpfully. 'You won't get one inside the lift.'

'Fine!' she spat. 'I'll ring when we get to the suite.'

He nodded. 'That would work.'

Pausing, he turned and opened a small door in the side of the lift, slid a card into it and swiped it down.

'Only we're not going to the suite.'

The lift stopped moving.

Addie stared at him incredulously.

'Have you lost your mind?' she said finally. 'Why are you doing this?'

'I told you. We didn't finish our conversation.'

'There is nothing else to talk about,' she said furiously. 'Why do you think I left? I don't have anything to say to you.'

He nodded. 'I know. And you don't have to say anything. You just have to listen. I'll do all the talking.'

'It's too late, Malachi. If you wanted to talk to me you should have done it an hour ago.' Her eyes narrowed. 'In fact you should have done it five years ago.'

He leaned back against the doors, his face hardening. 'As I recall, you didn't give me a chance.'

She stepped towards him, her fingers curling into fists. 'That is *not* what happened. I tried to talk to you and you just walked away.'

'It was our *wedding*!' His face was taut. 'You were making—'

'What? A scene? Oh, I'm sorry—what was I supposed to do? I'd just heard two men talking about how lucky it was that your new wife had such strong ties with the local community. How it had made such a difference to getting your plans for a new casino approved.'

'That's not what happened,' he said savagely, and he stepped towards her, his eyes locking on to hers.

'So that *isn't* why you married me?' Her whole body was shaking with anger but her heart contracted painfully at the memory. 'Tell me I got it wrong. Go on. Tell me.'

Looking at his stricken face, she felt suddenly nauseous.

'You can't because it's true.'

'No.' His voice echoed loudly around the lift. 'I admit when I asked you to marry me I thought it would be good for business.' Tipping his head back, he breathed out sharply, his face twisting. 'But then things changed. I started to care about you—'

He took a step forward and with shock she saw that his hands were shaking.

'I missed you when you weren't there and I looked forward to seeing you.' He shook his head vehemently, his eyes dropping away. 'You have to understand, Addie. I'd never felt like that before. I didn't know what I was feeling.'

She looked up at him uncertainly. 'What *were* you feeling?'

He shivered. 'Out of control. Scared.'

She bit her lip. 'Why were you scared?'

He clenched his teeth. 'Because I cared. About you. Only I didn't know how to deal with those feelings. When you got so upset it hurt to see you like that and I just wanted to get away. I didn't think you would leave—'

'I didn't think there was any point in staying,' she said flatly. 'I thought you didn't love me.'

His eyes met hers. 'I can see why you would think that.' Looking away, he ran a hand over his face. 'I grew up not knowing what love was. I didn't understand how to love someone or be loved. I didn't have relationships. I had sex. And sex was just a way of feeling things without actually having to care.'

His voice cracked.

'When I met you that changed. I started to see the world differently. But it was still all so new, and I found it hard.' He shook his head. 'I should have come after you.'

There was a lump in her throat. 'I was to blame too.' She bit her lip. 'I should have stayed and fought for our marriage.'

He breathed out slowly. 'Upstairs, you said you loved me and that you wanted to try again. Was that true?'

Hesitating, she stared at him in silence. But she knew the truth was written all over her face anyway. 'Yes. But I won't be your mistress, Malachi.'

He shook his head, his eyes damp, his face pale and strained. 'I don't want you to be my mistress.' Reaching out, he gently took hold of her hands in his. 'But I *do* want you to forgive me for blackmailing you. And treating you so badly.'

His hands tightened around hers.

'I'm so sorry, Addie. I know I don't deserve you, and I should have let you go tonight. Let you find someone kinder and better than me. But I can't. I know it's selfish, but I can't allow you to leave because I love you. And my life is nothing without you.'

Breathing out unsteadily, she looked down at his hands. 'Does that mean you're not going to sue me?' she said softly.

He shook his head. 'It wasn't a binding contract.'

She smiled weakly and then pulled away slightly. 'What about divorcing me?'

She felt her heart tumble over as he shook his head.

'Absolutely not.' Gently, he pulled her towards him. 'You're not getting rid of me that easily. You're my wife, and as soon as we get out of here I'm telling the entire world.'

She looked up at him, her mouth trembling. 'I don't know, Malachi. It all sounds perfect in here. But we can't stay in a lift for the rest of our lives.'

He grinned. 'It's tempting, but—trust me, sweet-heart. I can make this work.' He frowned. 'Which is more than can be said for this lift…'

Her eyes narrowed. 'You broke the lift?'

He nodded. 'It would appear so. See that flashing light—that means it's locked.'

'Locked!'

He gave a helpless shrug. 'I was a little distracted.'

'So what happens next?' she asked slowly.

His eyes dropped to her mouth. 'We have to wait. Just for a couple of hours.'

She lifted an eyebrow. 'I see. I suppose we'll just have to think of a way to pass the time.'

His hands slid slowly round her waist. 'Do you have any ideas?

'Actually, I do.' She wrapped her arms around his neck and kissed him gently on the lips.

He drew away from her, his eyes softening. 'Me too.' Lowering his mouth, he brushed his lips across hers. 'Did I tell you that I love you, Mrs King?'

His hands moved over her waist, sliding under the shirt, warm palms touching her bare skin, and she felt her heart start to race.

'Yes, you did.' She closed her eyes. 'But tell me again.'

* * * * *

If you enjoyed this story,
check out these other great reads from
Louise Fuller:
VOWS MADE IN SECRET
A DEAL SEALED BY PASSION
Available now!

#3457 TO BLACKMAIL A DI SIONE
The Billionaire's Legacy
by Rachael Thomas

Liev Dragunov's spent a lifetime plotting revenge against the Di Siones, and having Bianca's bracelet makes her perfect for his plan. Bianca must become his fake fiancée—but when Liev discovers her innocence, desire becomes sweeter than revenge...

#3458 DEMETRIOU DEMANDS HIS CHILD
Secret Heirs of Billionaires
by Kate Hewitt

Alekos Demetriou gave Iolanthe Petrakis one sinfully seductive night, never knowing that his enemy's daughter left carrying his child. Ten years later, after discovering Iolanthe's secret, Alekos declares he will legitimize his son—and that they *will* marry!

#3459 THE SHEIKH'S BABY SCANDAL
One Night With Consequences
by Carol Marinelli

Playboy sheikh Kedah Al Quasim has spent years behaving outrageously; now he must accept his royal duty and marry. His coolly beautiful assistant, Felicia Hamilton, seems the perfect distraction, but Kedah isn't prepared for the scandalous consequence: Felicia pregnant with his baby!

#3460 A RING FOR VINCENZO'S HEIR
One Night With Consequences
by Jennie Lucas

Impoverished Scarlett Ravenwood has no choice but to interrupt wealthy Vincenzo Borgia's wedding—she needs his help protecting their unborn child! To claim his heir, Vincenzo has no choice but to marry Scarlett. She suddenly has everything—except his heart!

HPCNM0816RA

#3461 TRAPPED BY VIALLI'S VOWS
Wedlocked!
by Chantelle Shaw
Waitress Marnie Clarke refuses to be Leandro Vialli's "dirty little secret," and flees, secretly pregnant. After a paternity test proves his fatherhood, Leandro must claim his heir—and when an accident steals Marnie's memories, he makes her believe they're engaged!

#3462 THE SECRET BENEATH THE VEIL
by Dani Collins
Mikolas Petrides will secure a business deal in marriage. But when he lifts the veil, he finds his intended's protective sister—Viveka Brice! With the marriage canceled, Viveka must compensate Mikolos somehow—and he's determined to make her his *mistress*.

#3463 DEFYING THE BILLIONAIRE'S COMMAND
by Michelle Conder
Dare James is furious that some woman has gotten her claws into his grandfather—but when he confronts the family doctor, she's unexpectedly attractive. Carly is no gold digger, and she can't wait to wipe the smile from Dare's handsome face!

#3464 THE MISTRESS THAT TAMED DE SANTIS
The Throne of San Felipe
by Natalie Anderson
An unexpected encounter with notorious temptress Bella Sanchez has Prince Antonio De Santis breaking his rules about women. Antonio's entrance shakes up Bella's empty life, and she can't resist a forbidden affair. But can she tame the De Santis prince?

REQUEST YOUR FREE BOOKS!

HARLEQUIN

Presents®

2 FREE NOVELS PLUS
2 FREE GIFTS!

PASSION GUARANTEED SEDUCTION

YES! Please send me 2 FREE Harlequin Presents® novels and my 2 FREE gifts (gifts are worth about $10). After receiving them, if I don't wish to receive any more books, I can return the shipping statement marked "cancel." If I don't cancel, I will receive 6 brand-new novels every month and be billed just $4.30 per book in the U.S. or $5.24 per book in Canada. That's a saving of at least 13% off the cover price! It's quite a bargain! Shipping and handling is just 50¢ per book in the U.S. and 75¢ per book in Canada.* I understand that accepting the 2 free books and gifts places me under no obligation to buy anything. I can always return a shipment and cancel at any time. Even if I never buy another book, the two free books and gifts are mine to keep forever.

106/306 HDN GHRP

Name _____
(PLEASE PRINT)

Address _____ Apt. # _____

City _____ State/Prov. _____ Zip/Postal Code _____

Signature (if under 18, a parent or guardian must sign) _____

Mail to the **Reader Service:**
IN U.S.A.: P.O. Box 1867, Buffalo, NY 14240-1867
IN CANADA: P.O. Box 609, Fort Erie, Ontario L2A 5X3

**Are you a current subscriber to Harlequin Presents® books
and want to receive the larger-print edition?
Call 1-800-873-8635 or visit www.ReaderService.com.**

* Terms and prices subject to change without notice. Prices do not include applicable taxes. Sales tax applicable in N.Y. Canadian residents will be charged applicable taxes. Offer not valid in Quebec. This offer is limited to one order per household. Not valid for current subscribers to Harlequin Presents books. All orders subject to credit approval. Credit or debit balances in a customer's account(s) may be offset by any other outstanding balance owed by or to the customer. Please allow 4 to 6 weeks for delivery. Offer available while quantities last.

Your Privacy—The Reader Service is committed to protecting your privacy. Our Privacy Policy is available online at www.ReaderService.com or upon request from the Reader Service.

We make a portion of our mailing list available to reputable third parties that offer products we believe may interest you. If you prefer that we not exchange your name with third parties, or if you wish to clarify or modify your communication preferences, please visit us at www.ReaderService.com/consumerchoice or write to us at Reader Service Preference Service, P.O. Box 9062, Buffalo, NY 14240-9062. Include your complete name and address.

HP15

"If you want to stand any chance of getting your precious bracelet back, we will become engaged." Liev said the words so softly, all but whispering them in her ear, that to anyone watching they would have looked like lovers. She backed away, bumping into someone passing behind her. She didn't apologize. She couldn't speak. All she could think of was his cruel terms.

"I have no intention of becoming engaged and certainly not to a man like you." She glared angrily at him, totally shocked he could even be suggesting such a thing just to gain entry into a world he was obviously not born into. A world he didn't belong to.

"A man like me? A thief and a nobody?" Liev snarled the words at her, his voice a low growl, laced with menace.

Bianca lifted her chin, not wanting to show him her fear. "That's not what I meant and you know it."

"For your information, if I had a choice, I would not be engaged to a spoiled little rich girl such as yourself."

She smarted at his inference that she was materialistic and counted every last gem and diamond she owned. It was so far from the truth it was laughable, but right now she couldn't laugh.

"We can never be engaged. I won't do it."

"Then you will not be able to add the bracelet to your collection of trinkets." He raised his brows and a cruel smile spread over his lips.

"You purposefully bid for something I wanted just to satisfy your own greed?"

"Yes." He wasn't at all shamed by her statement—if anything he was proud of it.

"That's blackmail." She raged against him and the injustice of it all. What was she going to tell her grandfather now?

"Not blackmail, Ms. Di Sione. Business. Now do we have a deal?"

Don't miss
TO BLACKMAIL A DI SIONE by Rachael Thomas,
available September 2016 wherever
Harlequin Presents® books and ebooks are sold.

www.Harlequin.com

JUST CAN'T GET ENOUGH
OF THE ALPHA MALE?
Us either!

Come join us at **I Heart Presents** to hear the
latest from your favorite Harlequin Presents
authors and get special behind-the-scenes secrets
of the Presents team!

With access to the latest breaking news and
special promotions, **I Heart Presents** is *the*
destination for all things Presents. Get up close
and personal with the sexy alpha heroes who
make your heart beat faster and share your love
of these glitzy, glamorous reads with the authors,
the editors and fellow Presents fans!